Reviews for

# Memoirs of a Dangerous Alien

'Never a dull moment!' *The Independent on Sunday*

'An accessible page turner of unusual quality ... a substantial adventure story, funny and observant' *The Sunday Times*

'Fast-moving and funny' *SHE*

'One of the most exciting children's books I've read in a long time' *Books For Keeps*

'Exciting and racy, an unputdownable read' Mind Boggling Books judges

'Really exciting with lots of twists and surprises ... I simply couldn't put it down and I ended up reading it in one night' Mark Ashton for Lancashire County Library Children's Book of the Year

# Pulling the Plug on the Universe

## maggie prince

A Dolphin
Paperback

Published in paperback in 1996
by Orion Children's Books
a division of the Orion Publishing Group Ltd
Orion House
5 Upper St Martin's Lane
London WC2H 9EA

First published in Great Britain in 1995
by Orion Children's Books

This edition published in 2000

A catalogue record for this book
is available from the British Library

Printed in Great Britain by Clays Ltd, St Ives plc

ISBN 1 85881 270 4

For Jean Marie Prince
with love and thanks

# Minus One

It is dark and I am sitting on a wall in Somerset. It is almost like being indoors because the storm clouds are low overhead and the darkness is like walls around me. There is muffled thunder in the distance. In a moment I shall be getting very wet indeed, but there is a little time left and a little light from the torch which I am shining on this, the second of my hardbacked grey notebooks.

If you haven't read *Memoirs of a Dangerous Alien* perhaps I should explain. Four months ago the world stumbled to the brink of oblivion. Aliens, led by the United Council of Planets, almost destroyed civilisation on Earth by brainwashing our world leaders into the use of fusion bombs. We are all still recovering.

I would not normally choose to sit in a dark garden to write, but frankly the atmosphere in the house is pretty tense these days. Mum seems to say nothing but, 'Dominic, you are not to have anything more to do with the Black Star Gang.' Dad rubs his hands across his face and glowers and says, 'Don't let me catch you going off into space again, my lad, not ever. Do you hear me?' It would be difficult not to, since his decibel count is rising steadily.

My younger sister, Julia, on the other hand, pesters to be allowed to help me 'save the universe' as she puts it. She could hardly do a worse job than I've been doing.

Worst of all, Auntie, my Great-aunt Veronica, currently assumes that all visitors to the house are dangerous aliens, so she slams the door in their faces, regardless of whether they are my friends from school, somebody selling double glazing or the vicar collecting for the church roof fund. I'm afraid the vicar is currently going round with a plaster on his nose since unfortunately his reflexes are slower than Auntie's.

It would be laughable if it were not all so dire, and if matters were not really so serious.

What you had better understand first of all is that most inhabitants of the universe are brainwashed. Oh, not you personally, I hope. If you are, then it means I have failed. Though how would you know if you were, I wonder?

Anyway, so far, as I write this and struggle against a sharp wind which is riffling the pages, Earth has been spared the mass mind-control of the United Council of Planets. What I and other members of the Black Star Gang would like to do is keep it that way.

I am writing this now, but I shall write no more until it is all over. I can feel that things will start happening again soon. I know that I shall have to go into space and find my friends Fenella, Mitzalie and Claude, all of them aliens, all of them Black Star Gang members, all of them wanted outlaws on the run. I know too that I must find my school's old computer teacher, Mr Batworthy, whom the aliens are also hunting, and who may have the key to the United Council of Planets' ominous interest in Earth.

It is a stormy summer night in the first quarter of the twenty-first century AD, and the rain has just started falling.

# One

'Dominic, they're aliens and they've gone. Fenella's an alien. You've got to accept it. They no longer have anything to do with us. It's all over.'

Peter and I were sitting in the sunshine on the back terrace of my house. Summer term had ended the previous week. It had been a strange term, with everyone so unnerved by the precarious international situation that concentration was difficult for teachers as well as students.

I looked across at my friend. He had taken to wearing a long, heavy, army greatcoat even in the hot weather, and had cut his red hair to a velvet stubble. He had altered his appearance as if he felt the need to be in disguise. I could hardly blame him after all that we had been through, pursued by agents of the United Council of Planets and almost brainwashed.

'He's having a teenage identity crisis,' I heard his mother telling my mother one day as they sat in the kitchen with shopping bags at their feet and brandy glasses in their hands. I knew, though, that it was more of an inter-planetary crisis that Peter was having, and that we were both having it.

'You don't mean that,' I said mildly in reply to his remarks. 'Why don't you take your coat off?' I leant back and let the sunlight filter between my eyelashes. I heard Peter's deckchair creak.

'There's not much we can do without transport anyway.' His voice was edgy. 'Since the aliens took all their gravity-blasters with them when they went, we couldn't go into space even if we wanted to.'

I sat up again and watched a strange cat on next door's wall. It was pale grey and was, in its turn, watching a wood pigeon which teetered along the edge of the terrace near our feet. I held out a small piece of biscuit to the pigeon. It waddled over. I wondered if flying was more exciting than walking for pigeons, and thought, with a surprising stab of nostalgia, of the terrifying days not so long ago when we had travelled faster than the speed of light in the Black Star Gang's tiny spaceships.

'I wonder if the aliens got old Batworthy,' said Peter with his eyes shut and his coat now draped over him like a blanket. 'They were certainly desperate enough to.'

'If they didn't, I wonder where he is now. He'd want to get back to his computers at the school, but there's been no sign of him, has there? I suppose he actually could go back now that all the aliens have gone.'

I looked beyond the high red-brick garden wall to the Old Rectory next door, where Fenella and her uncle had lived. The garden of the Old Rectory was overgrown now and the house itself had an air of neglect. The cat had settled down on the wall to watch us.

'You know, I'm tempted to go in there,' I said. Peter sat up abruptly and the pigeon lumbered off in alarm. 'Just to have a look around, you know, see if there's anything interesting they've left behind.' I stood up and walked towards the wall. 'Hello cat. Where did you come from?'

Peter groaned and pulled his coat over his head. 'You're mad,' he said in a muffled voice. 'Every time you've gone into the Old Rectory you've ended up in trouble.'

I ignored him, putting out my hand to the cat. It had unusual pinkish shading on its long thick fur, and circular bright green eyes in its flat face. 'My parents are going on holiday next week. That would give us a good opportunity.' I glanced back over my shoulder at Peter. He looked away coldly.

'Forget the "us" bit, Dominic. I'm not doing any breaking and entering. So who's going to be with you while your parents are away? Surely not just your great-aunt?'

'Oh no. Her sister's coming. Granny Probity.'

'Is she like your auntie?' Eccentric, Peter meant, but was too polite to say.

'Not really. Peter, come and look at this interesting

cat. It must be a very rare breed. I've never seen it round here before. Do you know whose it is?' I touched the cat's fur. It was amazingly fine, like thistledown. I stroked it gently. The cat pushed its face into my hand and said 'beep'.

# Two

Whereas Auntie was thin and crazy, her sister, Granny Probity, was fat and sane. On the morning my parents went on holiday we all stood on the step and waved to them as their car disappeared up the lane. Perkin and Maureen, our two cats, wove in and out of our legs, excited by all the coming and going.

'Well, that's them out of the way.' Granny Probity rubbed her hands together. 'Now we can all get down to enjoying ourselves.' She gave me a big kiss on the cheek. MWAH! it went, deafeningly, next to my ear. 'Let's all go and have a beer!' she shouted.

My parents were going to stay in Granny Probity's house in Yorkshire while she stayed with us in Somerset. 'I hope they manage to end up in the right place,' Granny Probity went on, glancing at her sister. This was a hidden reference to the time Auntie had forgotten where she was going and ended up in Edinburgh. Auntie sighed and took a bottle of tranquillisers out of her cardigan pocket.

Granny Probity adjusted her glasses and peered up the lane to where Peter had just turned the corner and was heading this way. 'Who's yon, in the horseblanket and the crewcut?' she demanded.

Auntie crammed a couple of tranquillisers into her mouth. 'It's one of Dominic's friends, Probity. He's having an adolescent crisis. Now come on in. I'm going to put the kettle on.'

Granny Probity made a noise of explosive scorn. 'Adolescence! Nobody had adolescence when I was a girl! We didn't have time!' She followed her sister into the house. 'I brought my cricket kit. We can have cricket practice after lunch.'

Auntie's sigh was audible all the way from the kitchen.

Peter reached the front door and I smiled at him, then glanced at the Old Rectory next door.

'It's as good a time as any, Peter. Those two will have a lot to talk about and Julia's going over to her friend's house.'

Peter pulled his coat more closely around him. His face was red and shiny from the heat. 'Come on then.' To my surprise he started to slouch back down the drive towards the lane. I followed him quickly, covering my astonishment at his agreement and feeling a sudden surge of optimism. Perhaps Peter was actually starting to feel better. He looked around the verge where foxgloves nestled into the hedge and young blackbirds were piping softly. 'Have you seen that weird beeping cat again?' he enquired.

I shook my head. We turned in at the Old Rectory gate. I noticed how run to seed the flowerbeds and shrubbery were. The sun was hot on my back through my t-shirt. The raised voices of Auntie and Granny Probity drifted over from next door.

I felt no guilt at breaking in. No one had lived here for months now.

'Let's walk right round the house and see if any windows are open,' I suggested. 'The aliens left in such a hurry that they might not have had time to lock up properly.' Memories came rushing back uninvited as we moved slowly round the large, grey house. I remembered the corpse in the cupboard, Fenella pointing a gun at my head, gravity-blasters spinning out of time and space into hypervortex to jump across the universe faster than light. Did I want all that again? Did we really have to go on with this? Did we even have to stay in the Black Star Gang at all? But then, if not us, who?

In the back garden the weeds had run riot. The windows of the house looked dirty and the ivy which grew up the walls was sending small tendrils across the windows too. In the kitchen window one pane was cracked. I indicated this to Peter.

'That might be a way in.'

'Beep.'

We both jumped.

'Beep beep.' Something lurched out of the shrubbery and slung itself affectionately against our legs.

'Hello cat.' I bent down in amusement. 'What are you doing here? Where do you live?' I looked up at Peter. 'I wonder if it's a stray. It feels rather thin under all this fur.'

Peter bent down too and stroked the cat.

'I've never heard a cat make that sort of noise before. It's probably some peculiar foreign breed.'

'Maybe we should feed it. I can't very well take it home because Perkin and Maureen would be jealous.'

Peter picked the cat up and held it against his cheek. 'I'll give it some food over at the farm. Let's forget this stupid breaking-in idea and just go and feed the cat.'

I shook my head and grasped his arm.

'Come on Peter. We've got this far.' Cautiously I pressed my hand against the broken pane of the kitchen window. It shifted slightly and a small piece of glass fell into the sink. I took off my t-shirt and wrapped my hand in it, then carefully held the broken edge of glass and manoeuvred it to and fro. It started to ease out of the frame. Five minutes later I was able to reach my hand in and lift the latch on the kitchen window.

The house smelt stale inside. In the kitchen the worktop surfaces were clean and empty. From force of habit I opened the fridge and we surveyed some mouldering cheese, a putrefied lettuce and a half bottle of greenish milk, with distaste.

In the hall a pile of mail lay on the polished wooden

floor. I found I wanted to keep looking over my shoulder. When something brushed my ankle I nearly collapsed. The beeping cat had followed us in.

We went upstairs. The doors were all closed. Slightly nervous, I turned the tarnished brass doorknob of Fenella's room. I knew it was ridiculous to look for a note. There would have been no time for notes as she fled from the clutches of the armed guards.

Peter was watching me. I shrugged.

'I don't know what I'm looking for but it's worth looking. You never know. There may be something that would help us contact them. The communicators are no good now.' I touched my ear which still contained the fine sliver of metal which had once been my means of contacting other Black Star members.

Feeling hesitant, I began to search. The beeping cat found a ribbon hanging from a drawer and began smacking it to and fro playfully. I looked among the school papers in Fenella's desk, feeling very uncomfortable about doing this.

'I'll search Uncle Simon's room,' said Peter. 'It would help if we knew what we were looking for.'

Suddenly the cat's ears pricked up.

'Wait,' I whispered, and pointed to the cat. Peter's eyes widened as he saw the animal turn to watch the door.

'Oh no, it can hear something.'

Then we heard it too. From downstairs there came a soft rasping sound.

# Three

It was a key turning in a lock. It sounded like the front door lock. My first thought was Fenella, but the heavy footsteps which followed the opening of the door told me it was definitely not her. Peter and I looked at each other in silence. We both looked at the cat and I willed it not to beep.

'It could be an estate agent showing someone round,' mouthed Peter.

Shoes squeaked on the wooden floor of the hall. Suddenly we heard the front door slam back against the wall and the knocker clap loudly.

'I can't stand this Earth heat!' snapped a petulant male voice. 'Let's get this over and done with quickly for goodness' sake.'

'Look, if it were up to me we'd be home already, Barty. It's you who insisted on staying to look for your blasted cat. Only a complete idiot would bring his cat on an intergalactic mission. Anyway, they do have

13

*quarantine* regulations here, you know.' It was another male voice.

I felt my limbs go weak with fright. I saw Peter's hands clench. The two intruders were speaking the interplanetary language.

The cat stood up and moved quickly towards the open bedroom door. I watched it with relief, but then it paused and glanced back at us. I flapped my hands at it.

'Go on. Good cat. Goodbye.'

It ran towards me in delight. Obviously it thought this hand-flapping was a great game. I could hear the two aliens moving round the downstairs rooms now.

'Well, the stupid animal's obviously not here, Barty.'

'I'm not so sure. It could easily have got in through that broken window. It's exactly the sort of place that Positron would go. He's like that. He loves getting into tiny spaces. I'm going to look upstairs. There's no way I'm going back to Hamshoma without my cat.'

Peter and I glanced round in panic. One pair of footsteps was on the stairs now. The treads creaked noisily.

'Positron!' We jumped as the alien's voice came from right outside the room where we stood. The open door hid us, but it would only need the alien to step into the room and we would be in full view. To my relief the cat rushed out, beeping excitedly. I held my breath.

'Oh *Positron*! You bad cat!' The tones were indulgent. 'Scupper! He's here. I've found him!'

Go go go, I urged them silently. Just take your stupid

cat and go away. But instead, the second pair of footsteps mounted the stairs too.

'Well, thank goodness for that. You'd better just hang on to him while I search up here for anything those irritating Black Star people might have left behind.'

I felt as if I had been punched. They were on the same mission as we were.

One pair of footsteps returned downstairs and I could hear the cat's beeping becoming fainter. 'I'll put him in the gravity-blaster, then I'll search downstairs, Scupper,' called Barty's voice.

Carefully I moved over to the window, looking for their gravity-blaster. It was nowhere in sight.

I wondered if it might be possible for us to climb quietly down from the window and escape, then realised that with one alien upstairs and one downstairs, both searching, our chances of remaining undiscovered were negligible. If we were found, I knew without doubt what the result would be. We would be brain-processed and our minds wiped clean of everything the aliens found undesirable.

The drop from the window was sheer, anyway. The ivy was thin here and would not support us. There was no convenient drainpipe and no sloping roof. There was no way we could get down without making a lot of noise and possibly breaking a limb. Peter looked out too, then turned away, rolling his eyes in despair. In mid roll he stopped. The effect was grotesque.

For several moments he stood still, staring at the

15

ceiling. My gaze followed his. Then I saw what he had seen. There was a trapdoor in the ceiling of Fenella's room.

We looked at each other.

'It must lead to the loft,' I whispered.

Peter nodded. In the rest of the house we could now hear clatterings and rattlings. The aliens were still searching.

Suddenly filled with hope, I looked round for some way of opening the loft door. It had a pull-ring and looked like the sort of trapdoor that would have a descending ladder on the back of it. I seized a chair from next to Fenella's dressing table and placed it under the trapdoor, then climbed on to it. It wasn't quite high enough so I stepped down again and placed a leather footrest on top of the chair, then climbed back up the whole wobbly edifice.

Outside, alien footsteps were on the landing once more. They sounded terrifyingly close. I took hold of the ring fastener and pulled. The catch made a loud click.

'Hey! Barty! What was that?' The footsteps on the landing paused, and there was a listening silence. I tried to ease the trapdoor open slowly, realising we had only moments now to let down the ladder, put the chair and footrest innocently away, get ourselves into the loft and pull the ladder up again. It was clearly impossible and in the moment that I realised it was impossible, gravity took over. As the trapdoor opened past a certain point it pushed me off balance and swung down. The wooden ladder attached to the back of it unfolded with a rush and hit me on the head. I fell to the floor. The noise was tremendous. Footsteps rushed along the landing.

'Barty! Barty! Come up here!' yelled Scupper's voice.

With impressive reflexes Peter slammed the bedroom door and rammed the fallen chair under its handle. I struggled to my feet, gasping at a violent pain in my arm. Then we both pounded up the ladder and into the loft.

The bedroom door knob rattled furiously and something thudded on the wooden panels. In desperation we looked around in the dim loft. It had floorboards so it was easy to move around in. There was a light switch on one of the beams. Peter flicked it and the dusty roofspace was filled with brightness.

'Oh . . .'

I saw it first. Peter was busy pulling on the strong green cord which drew the ladder up after us. The sound of wood splintering came from the room below. I stood upright and stared at the sight which confronted me in the far corner of this stuffy attic room. The trapdoor pulled shut and Peter secured the green cord. Then he turned and saw it too.

It was a gravity-blaster.

We crossed to it. It was small and red, a two-seater, fast-looking and modern, the shape of a sleek, covered go-kart.

'Oh *yes*.' Peter's voice was awestruck.

'If only we had the means of getting it out.'

There were noises in the bedroom beneath us now. We looked around. Various boxes and trunks were stored in the loft.

'Let's put one of these over the trapdoor.' Peter started dragging at a heavy wooden trunk. I helped him with one hand, unable to use the other because of the pain in my arm. I wondered if it was broken. We lifted the trunk with difficulty on to the folded loft ladder.

'The mechanism won't work now.' Peter gave the trunk a last push and we straightened up.

'Fenella or Uncle Simon must have had some means of bringing this gravity-blaster in.' I shook my head in puzzlement.

'She could have assembled it in here. She was good at that sort of thing.'

We looked round despairingly for some sign of an exit. Below us there was a cracking, crunching sound. The two aliens seemed to be wrenching at the closed trapdoor now. To my dismay I saw it sag beneath the trunk. They were starting to pull it open. As I watched, the ladder mechanism twisted to one side.

'Come on out, whoever is in there! You might as well give yourselves up. We've got you trapped.' The petulant alien voice was calling from right up against the crack. 'You've nothing to fear from us if you come out peacefully,' it cajoled.

'Pull the other one,' muttered Peter.

I stared at the roof. 'I think there is a way out,' I whispered to Peter. 'Just look at those spots of light.'

Peter looked at where fine rays of sunshine came in through tiny holes in the roof. Tiny dust particles hung in the rays, and the intermittent leakages of light seemed almost to form three sides of a square. Another trapdoor? The wooden beams of the roof were different there too, more evenly grained, as if of different wood.

'Unfortunately,' I sighed, as heavy crashing sounded below us, 'there isn't time to find out. Get in.' I slid back the glass dome of the gravity-blaster and jumped into the pilot's seat. Peter looked at me in horror. A wrenching, grinding noise came from the trapdoor.

'Peter, these things are built to withstand *meteorites*. Get in.' I jabbed my good hand towards the passenger seat.

Peter got in. With a soft hum the glass dome closed and we fastened our safety belts. I muttered a brief prayer that granite roof tiles were not harder than meteorites, then pressed maximum upward thrust.

# Four

At breakfast time we had been in Somerset. By lunch-time we were in space.

The moment when we crashed through the roof of the Old Rectory was one of the most frightening of my life. For a moment I thought we hadn't made it, because the impact was so great and the noise so shattering.

Grey granite roof tiles whirled about the dome of the gravity-blaster, battering at its reinforced glass. The whole spacecraft juddered from side to side like a ship on a stormy sea, and it took me several minutes to right it and set it back on an even keel.

During all this time we must have been in full view of any resident of Stoke Stiley who happened to be around. I didn't wait to see. I flew us high over the Somerset Levels and programmed our small spacecraft to revolve faster and faster into hypervortex past the speed of light and away.

'The Somerset flying saucer will probably go down in history,' remarked Peter when the nauseating rotation was over and dazzling, unresisting space streamed by. I spoke to the spacecraft's computer and gave it a list of co-ordinates. Peter looked at me with a start.

'What are those? Where are we going? I thought we'd just cruise around a bit and then go home.'

The computer spoke before I could.

'Co-ordinates for Planet Bench Hellezine confirmed. Estimated time of arrival outside the city of Stot one hour and twenty minutes.'

'Dominic!' Peter shouted. 'What on earth have you done?'

I programmed a Coke from the drinks machine in the wall and handed it to Peter. 'Those are the co-ordinates that a Black Star member gave me when I was escaping from the Alpha Centauri Interchange at Easter. It's where Fenella, Claude and Mitzalie probably went when they first escaped from Earth.'

Peter looked at me furiously. 'Dominic, are you mad? There's nothing you can do for them that they can't do twenty times better for themselves. They won't still be there. They'll have moved on. They *are* on the run, you know.'

My arm was very painful. I arranged it carefully on the armrest.

'Look, Peter, we couldn't go home yet anyway, not with those aliens still in the neighbourhood. Let's just see where Fenella and the others landed. All I want to do is see what sort of a place it is, then we'll go home. I promise.'

Peter gave me a resigned look.

'Let's try and get some interplanetary news on the receiver,' I suggested, touching a button. There was a loud crackle and a voice came on, speaking the interplanetary language. I programmed myself a fizzy apple juice and we settled back.

'. . . and that ends today's programme on space station gardening. Next week, the effects of zero gravity on greenfly. Now it's time for the news with Melly Brant . . .'

Peter and I listened, transfixed. It was unbelievable to be hearing voices from other planets again, after all these months.

'Our main headlines today are once again the fire at the gravity-blaster factory on the planet Myria . . .'

I remembered the Myrions, disruptive giants with pale greenish skins, who disagreed with the United Council of Planets and their oppressive regime, but whose bumbling methods did more harm that good.

'. . . and police say that sabotage has not been ruled out. Three members of the workforce are being questioned by computer.

'At the Alpha Centauri Interchange, staff are ending their three month tour of duty and celebrating with extra vitamin tablets in the computer room. Replacement staff will be arriving from Interplanetary Headquarters later today.

'And finally, the infamous physicist Ista Frith, previously a member of the Council of Planets but recently revealed to be leader of the iniquitous Black Star Gang, finished her brain-processing today. Programmers say her brain is now fully rehabilitated and she will take her place once more as a useful member of society. Council sources suggest that Frith is expected to take up work as a rat catcher on the planet Hamshoma . . .'

I slumped back in my seat. I had known about Ista Frith's capture. I had heard it over my communicator while it was happening. BS One was the name by which we had known her. (We all had secret identification numbers. I was BS Eight and Peter was BS Nine.) To know that BS One's brain was now blanked out, to know that her ingenuity was gone, that her astonishing inventiveness in making the gadgets which Black Star members used to protect themselves, was no longer there, was almost unbearable. She had been fed into a computer and her individuality had been deleted.

Peter too looked upset.

'Somehow I had hoped she would get away,' he said.

I nodded, thinking about BS One and our other friends in the Black Star Gang. 'I wonder who is left,' I whispered. 'There may not actually be many of us.'

# Five

'We'd better get some more information about this planet we're heading for,' I said, and activated the voice control of the computer.

'Computer, do you have any information about the planet Bench Hellezine?'

The computer gave a sniff. I stared at it in astonishment, thinking I must have misinterpreted the sound. Then it spoke. 'Just because I've been stuck in a loft for three months doesn't mean I'm totally out of touch, you know.'

Peter and I both gaped at the machine. I was about to speak but the computer clearly had not finished yet.

'I'm actually Fenella Summerling's computer, anyway, so I don't really think I have to tell you anything. Not that anyone cares what a computer feels. I'm sure I don't know what you're doing here. No one bothers to tell me anything. Fenella went off without a word of goodbye . . .' The computer's metallic voice was sounding more and more upset. 'It's so thoughtless. Fenella had programmed me in *special ways*. Nothing you would understand, of course . . .' Its voice trailed away.

'Oh dear,' Peter whispered. 'A computer that's having a nervous breakdown.' He raised his voice again. 'How do you mean, Fenella had programmed you in special ways?'

The computer was silent for a moment.

'I couldn't possibly say,' it eventually replied in a prim tone.

'We're friends of Fenella, too,' I said to it. There was another pause.

'Well, bad luck. I don't suppose she said goodbye to you either.'

'Oh dear, the poor thing's feelings are really hurt.' Peter kept his voice low, but not low enough.

'I don't need your sympathy!' There was obviously nothing wrong with the computer's hearing. 'Just don't do anything else stupid like going through roofs. *And* another thing, you don't seem to be aware that this gravity-blaster is fitted with one of the new invisibility screens, so I suggest you use it next time instead of making such an exhibition of yourselves. It's the button on the far left.'

I loosened my seat belt and sat forward in my seat.

'Thank you.' I glanced at the button. It did say 'invisibility screen'. This was something new. Alien technology never failed to astound me. I thought for a moment and then spoke to the computer again. 'Listen, computer, we need your co-operation. Do you have a name?'

'Nothing I intend telling you.'

Peter sighed, but I had had a sudden thought.

'Computer, my name is Dominic. Didn't we meet once before aboard the Starship Ashkey?' These were the secret passwords of the Black Star Gang. Softly, inside the computer, something gave a faint click, then without my touching it the display screen came on. The metallic voice spoke again.

'That's different then, Dominic. Perhaps we did and perhaps we didn't. I really wouldn't like to say. Anyway, my name is Newt, and information about Bench Hellezine is appearing on our screen right now.'

I was uncertain as to whether 'our' was supposed to indicate co-operation or royal status.

'Thank you.' I leaned forward again and studied the closely packed information on the screen. It was interspersed with maps, diagrams and low level aerial photographs. Bench Hellezine appeared to be a bleak place. It was a small planet about the size of Earth's moon, but pear-shaped and plagued by volcanoes and earthquakes. Its equatorial regions were barren and hot, its polar regions barren and cold. Its people were poor and lived on Council aid because more often than not their crops failed as a result of the harsh climate.

Newt spoke again just as Peter and I scrolled on to the last screenful of information.

'I'm taking us out of hypervortex. Bench Hellezine is

visible on your control screen and will be visible through the dome in five minutes. Solar flares can be seen on Bench Hellezine's sun, worth looking at if you like fireworks. Look out through the right side of the dome to see them. I find that my function is being affected by them.' I looked at the computer in alarm, then out through the right side of the glass dome over our heads. For a moment I couldn't speak. The sight was awesome.

Bench Hellezine's sun was an orange and blue star. Great columns of purple flame stood out all around it. The words that Peter spoke then, in a hushed voice, are not permitted by my publishers to be repeated here.

When Newt spoke again, his tones were distorted. I refer to it as him, which is ridiculous, I know, since it is a machine and not a person, but given the personality with which Fenella had programmed it, it was difficult to remember this.

For anyone who is wondering why I refer to it as him rather than her, there are two reasons. One is that the tones and cadences of its voice were masculine, and the other is because it sounded as if it were in love with Fenella.

'Two minutes to touchdown,' Newt informed us in these distorted tones. 'There are incapacitators in the cupboards at the back if you want them.'

I reached behind me and slid back a door of the small storage cupboard. It seemed a long time since I had seen one of these gun-shaped instruments which could temporarily paralyse or knock out an enemy. I took out both of them, complete with holsters, and handed one to Peter. I also took out a pair of solar powered binoculars.

The planet was clearly visible outside the dome now. It was indeed pear-shaped. It looked like a chunk of rock untidily hewn from the side of some mountain. Newt spoke again, with even worse dislocation in his voice.

'Dominic . . . Nodimic . . . it may be . . .' The voice died away on a hollow whine. Thoroughly alarmed now, I stabbed at the enhancer button. The voice came back in a ghostly bass croak. 'I hope you can fly this crate on manual, Micinod, because this force field is leaving me a little high. I must warn you . . . it may be . . . it may be that the other computers on this planet are similarly affected . . .' The voice sank and faded further. I pressed the enhancer button again. Peter had taken over flying the gravity-blaster on manual. A series of clicks came from within the computer.

The hollow booming whisper was almost impossible to decipher now, but what it sounded like was, 'The people of Bench Hellezine may not be correctly brain-processed, Mickey Mouse. They may be over-processed or not processed at all. Beware of them, Nickynoc, beware . . . they may be misprocessed to the point of mania . . .' Then Newt was silent.

A few moments later, we landed for the first time on an alien planet.

# Six

I shall never forget that scene for as long as I live. We emerged from our gravity-blaster and stood on the powdery soil of a foreign world. The air was feverishly hot, a brassy glare from a copper sun in a white sky, blue-tinged at times from the ferocious sunspots overhead.

It smelt strange too, the way that a different city or country smells strange. Faintly, the undertow was of sulphur.

'You'll never need space helmets on the planets,' Fenella had assured me once. 'As far as we know life has only developed on planets with a nitrogen and oxygen atmosphere like Earth's.'

So we breathed in the alien air and looked around at the alien landscape, and I thought of Fenella Brown, as I had known her, or Fenella Summerling, which seemed to be her real name. There had been times in the past when I had almost forgotten that she was an alien. I had believed that I knew her quite well. We had been friends, slightly more than friends as far as I was concerned. Now I wondered if I knew her at all.

I looked around. She could have landed here. She might have looked at this inhospitable landscape as I was doing now. Where would she and the other two have gone from here?

'They could be quite close,' I said to Peter.

Peter raised his eyebrows and looked around. 'You really think so, Dominic? Even if they did come here, that was months ago.'

We had landed on a hill, one of the few hills, it seemed, which was not a volcano. All around us truncated mountains stood in the distance. Their black and yellow smoke dimmed the horizon, giving it an unreal, indoor nearness. Around us the only shade was provided by rocks, huge heaps of granite-type boulders, gunmetal grey. The ground beneath our feet was grey and fluffy, looking like clumps of sheep's wool until we trod on it. Then it fell into powdery ash as though made of burnt tissue paper. Sparse wisps of grass grew half-heartedly in the shade of the rocks. There were no trees, and in a ring all around the horizon, the convoluted pavements of cooled volcanic lava marched away.

I nodded wearily in response to Peter's sceptical expression.

'I suppose not. Where would they have gone from here?'

But Peter was listening to something else. 'Shh.'

I heard it too, and raised the binoculars to my eyes.

The volcanoes leapt towards me, sweltering and blackened. The sound had been far off. It had sounded like a bell. I felt profound disquiet. The atmosphere on this planet did not inspire confidence.

'This is a dreadful place,' whispered Peter, clearly feeling the same. 'Has it occurred to you that we can hardly go wandering round foreign planets in Earth clothing?' He pulled his greatcoat closer around him.

I raised my hand to silence him. There was another sound, a different one. Unlikely as it seemed in this alien terrain, it was of hoofbeats. Peter frowned. Quickly we crouched down behind the nearest pile of boulders. The rocks were balanced on top of each other like children's bricks. I could see between them, and I realised that on the valley floor below us ran a road. It was from this that the sound came.

We watched, and in the distance a creature that looked like a large deer came into view, its hooves throwing up little puffs of ashy soil. As it drew nearer I saw that it had two large branched antlers on its head and a beard under its chin. Just below us the rider reined in and dismounted, tossing the reins over the animal's head with a careless flick that made it back away.

He started to climb the hill towards us. Peter and I glanced at each other in horror and I loosened my incapacitator in its holster. The man was sallow-skinned and sweating. He wore one of the normal interplanetary pyjamalike suits, but it was far more ornate than anything I had ever seen before, red with glittering gold embroidery. His shoulder length hair was black and his small black eyes looked like currants in a gingerbread man, thrown from a distance by someone with a bad aim.

Too late, I realised that although the gravity-blaster was behind a pile of boulders, it would be in full view of this stranger once he came a little further up the hill.

He stopped and looked around him.

'Where are you?' he called.

My heart gave a thud. Neither Peter nor I moved.

At that moment the alien rounded the pile of rocks and saw us.

'Good gracious! Whatever are you doing down there?' He stood with his hands on his hips and stared at us. Slowly we rose to our feet. His eyes swept us from head to foot. 'What *do* you look like? What in the world are you disguised as?'

I tried to find my voice. 'Oh . . . er . . . Earth people,' I croaked.

The alien hooted with laughter.

'Oh, very good. Brilliant. I'd forgotten that Hamshomis have the vestiges of a sense of humour. Well here we are with the papers.' He drew a large black envelope from his pocket. 'Oh my, the hair!' He flapped a hand at Peter's head. 'Wonderful! Where did you *get* all that wild gear, by the way?'

Peter appeared to have been struck dumb so I spoke again.

32

'The ... er ... Earth mission. It was ... er ... a complete shambles, but at least we got to keep the outfits.' I felt rather daring risking interplanetary slang. Although the language had been planted, whole, in our brains, by computer, we hadn't used it for several months.

The alien shook his head.

'Can't help feeling sorry for them. Still, we've got other things to worry about now. Here you are.' He handed the envelope over to me. With extreme caution I took it. Might this be a trick? Who was he and what were the papers to which he referred? More importantly, who did he think we were?

I remembered what Newt had said about brain-processing. There was something very odd about this man. Not only had he mentioned humour, a concept not much understood by the computerised brains of most of the alien universe, but he had also expressed an unconventional opinion, pity for what the inhabitants of Earth had gone through at alien hands. I glanced at Peter, wondering if he had noticed these things too. He had, because the next moment he addressed the alien.

'Didn't we meet once aboard the Starship Ashkey?'

I waited. If the man recognised these passwords of the Black Star Gang, then he might be a member, and his free-thinking attitude would be explained. Although there was always the risk now that Council agents might also know the passwords, since the capture of

Ista Frith and other Black Star members. We waited tensely for his reply.

He shrugged. 'Can't have been me, mate. I've never even heard of it.'

It was the wrong answer.

'I'll put the papers in the gravity-blaster,' I said, feeling disappointed as I walked over to our spacecraft. I pushed the envelope under my seat and closed the dome again.

'Well, I'd better get back.' The alien turned to walk down the hill. 'I'm glad you were early. I'm meeting my friend Fenella in half an hour.' He raised a hand and set off down the slope.

My strangled cry stopped him.

'What . . . ?'

Peter stepped in front of me. 'What name was that?' he enquired.

'Oh, my name? I'm so sorry. I thought the Science Foundation would have told you. Red Goff. My name is Red Goff. Yours of course are . . .'

'No.' I interrupted him. 'The other name. Did you say Fenella?'

'Steady, Dom. There are probably hundreds of Fenellas about,' muttered Peter under his breath.

The alien tilted his head and eyed me curiously, hands on his hips again. 'Do you know her? Fenella Summerling?'

I nodded. Red Goff shook his head and laughed.

'What an extraordinary coincidence. Well, we're

going to a concert later. Do you want to come along too?'

'Thank you. We'd be delighted.'

I heard Peter groan.

'Great.' The alien smiled. 'You're sure you have the time?'

'It's probably a trap.' Peter's voice was close to my ear. I ignored it.

'Yes, I think we have the time. We'll follow you by gravity-blaster. You go ahead.'

With a fast stride the alien set off back down the hill, leapt on to his mount and trotted away along the valley. We followed him in our gravity-blaster, hurdling gently over outcrops of boulders, with Peter grumbling all the way.

# Seven

The valley ran between the nearest row of volcanoes, and the walled city of Stot stood beyond them. A dry river bed crossed the valley and disappeared under the city walls.

As we travelled, I tried to obtain more information about the planet from Newt, but the screen simply showed the message 'Temporary inability to access information.'

Red Goff stopped before he reached the city walls and we came to a halt near him and rolled back the dome of the gravity-blaster.

'You'd better not take your spacecraft into the city,' he said. 'Parking's dreadful, and anyway vehicle thefts are commonplace these days, I'm afraid. There's a lot of unrest.'

I stared at him in amazement. Theft, in this regimented universe? Unrest? He saw my expression.

'It's since we drifted nearer to the sun and the computers went out. It's a sorry state of affairs when folks' brains can't be sorted out regularly. Which reminds me, you'd better keep the papers with you. Civilisation is on the skids, I fear.'

'Oh good,' murmured Peter very softly, but the alien heard him and gave him a sharp look. I changed the subject quickly and said something about the rock formations, but after that Red Goff kept glancing at us, and I started to share Peter's fear that this indeed might be a trap.

We entered Stot on foot, by the west gate, insofar as west had any meaning on this strange planet. I was surprised at the architecture we saw. Here was none of the streamlined modern glass and plastic such as we had seen at the Alpha Centauri Interchange. The walled city of Stot looked almost mediaeval.

There were narrow cobbled alleys with whitewashed houses, of which the upper storeys seemed to lean towards each other. Twisting streets turned unexpected corners and ended up in tiny courtyards. There were gentle arches and doors in walls. Hens and pigs ran along the gutters and people were shouting at each other. The smells were not all wholesome. Flies buzzed around unidentified heaps by the roadside.

The people looked as close to Earth people as I had seen among aliens. They wore clothing which resembled the standard interplanetary pyjama suits, but with startling variations such as scarves, jewellery and flowing sleeveless overgarments. In my Earth clothes, t-shirt and jeans, I felt less out of place than I had expected. Peter, in his army greatcoat, hardly looked out of place at all.

An old man tottered by. 'The end of the world is at hand,' he intoned.

'I daresay you're right,' replied Red Goff. 'I'm sure they won't let us go on like this for much longer.' He turned back to me. 'That's why we're so grateful to you for conveying our plan to the Science Foundation.'

He narrowed his eyes at me as we turned a corner. He had dismounted and was leading the animal now. 'You Hamshomis look awfully young to be doing this sort of thing. I suppose it's a sign of advancing age when interplanetary spies start to look young.'

I regarded him sceptically. He can't have been a great deal older than we were, maybe twenty at the most.

The next surprise was the ruins. The remains of some large building stood in a square, with trees at the far side and a rough wooden building constructed against the ruined wall. A bell tower rose up from the wall, and as we watched, the bell swayed and began to toll. This was what we had heard when we landed.

Ruins, where the United Council of Planets held sway? It hardly seemed possible. Red Goff stopped and looked at Peter and me. His deer nuzzled his shoulder and butted at him with its antlers. He tightened up the slack on its reins and rubbed its cheek.

'Yes, ruins, my friends. That's why . . . they came here. Perhaps I am saying too much. You see, as far as our lords and masters are concerned, Bench Hellezine is truly the back of beyond. They never even think of it, let alone imagine that anyone in their right mind would come here . . .' He stopped speaking. 'We shall see. This is where the concert is going to be held. I'll just go and see if I can find Fenella. Go in. We'll see you in the bar.' He clapped me on the shoulder and left us standing there.

There was a lot of noise coming from the wooden building, intermittent singing and loud laughter and the clashing of glasses. Peter touched the papers in his coat pocket.

'We must look at these as soon as we can, now that we've got rid of him,' he said. I nodded.

'I think we ought to go in here first and see what's happening, though.'

Peter followed me into the wooden building.

Inside, it was rather as one imagines an old-fashioned tavern. There were wooden benches and tables with people sprawling along and across them. There was a bar, and at the far end, a rough wooden stage. We stood at the back, ignored apart from a few curious glances at our clothes.

The room was full. The crowd seemed very good-natured apart from the old man who had followed us in and was trying to make someone care that the end of the world was at hand. There was an air of merriment and revelry here which I had not seen among aliens before. People were telling each other silly jokes and falling about laughing.

'I'm going to get us a couple of drinks,' I said after a few moments. Peter frowned at me.

'You do have to stay sober to save the universe, you know.'

'Orange juice or whatever equivalent they have here, idiot. I'll borrow some money off Red Goff if I can find him. Can I get you something?' I asked the old man.

'Allow me. I shall have no further use for money since the end of the world is at hand,' the ancient person replied in creaky tones. He accompanied me unsteadily to the bar.

But as we pushed our way through the crush of people the lights dimmed and the crowd quietened. Someone whistled and another person shouted. The atmosphere was much like that at an Earth rock concert. From behind the scenes music with a slow, strong beat started. An air of anticipation grew in the crowd, a rising up of energy all around me in the packed hall.

Then the warm-up music faded and spotlights flashed and focused on the stage. I hardly noticed the drink thrust into my hands by the old man. There was a gasp as something fell from the ceiling on to the stage. It was a musician in flowing black clothes and huge boots. He held a strange, triangular, stringed instrument. Other musicians in black rushed onstage from the wings and the real music began.

It was loud, fast and electronic. The crowd went mad, shouting, whistling and jumping. It was a release of all the energy that the waiting had created, a burst of euphoria. I had just about come to the conclusion that this band was really rather good when a door at the side of the stage at ground level opened and suddenly I wasn't hearing them any more.

Fenella stood there, at the bottom of the short flight of stairs that led to the stage. She was gazing back and forth across the crowd. She was dressed in blue and had her hands clasped in front of her. She radiated tight, nervous energy and was frowning. She had not seen me. I did nothing to attract her attention, but sat carefully on the edge of a wooden table and just watched her. The loud music went on somewhere in the background of my mind. I felt as though I too had been plugged in.

Peter struggled through the crowd to join me near the bar. He peered at me. 'Are you all right, Dominic?' He sounded slightly alarmed.

The old man handed him a drink. I drank some of mine. It tasted like lemonade but made my knees feel strange. I nodded my head in the direction of Fenella but Peter did not see her at first. He shook his head and frowned. 'What is it, Dom?' Then he saw her. I heard him gasp.

'It's her . . . I don't believe it . . .'

'Yes.'

'It's . . . it's too easy.' He rubbed a hand across his face as if to adjust his vision. 'I really don't believe it. I don't know what's in this drink, Dom, but . . .' He shook his head again. 'I mean . . . one leap into space and there she is, almost exactly where we landed? There must be a snag.'

'A snag,' repeated the old man. 'Well, you see, the end of the world is at hand.'

'She would have been given the same co-ordinates as us, Peter,' I replied. 'This is supposed to be a safe planet. It makes sense that we should meet up.'

The music changed. The next song was different. A girl singer sang on her own and the song was full of dangerous words like freedom. It was in a minor key and had a slow beat. The room went quiet.

'She's pushing her luck a bit,' whispered the old man, his mug of whatever it was half way to his lips. 'You never know who's listening.'

'Does it matter, if the end of the world is at hand?' I asked him.

The atmosphere in the room was very different now from that during the previous song. People appeared awkward. Some looked away and shuffled their feet. The drink was making my head feel weightless. I stood up from the table, because the song deserved it, and Fenella saw me.

# Eight

She faltered. Her arms fell to her sides and she looked visibly shocked. Then she was pushing her way across the room and moments later we were hugging each other.

The song ended. Only one person applauded. It was a remarkable contrast to the reception of the previous song. Then Peter started clapping, and so did Fenella and I, awkwardly entangled, then the old man started slapping his knee with his free hand and gradually the applause grew across the room. Faces around me looked guilty and surprised at their own daring.

'They were afraid to clap,' I whispered.

'She was singing about revolution.' They were the first words that Fenella had spoken to me since Easter. I found that I was very glad to hear her voice.

'Hello Fenella.'

'Hello Dominic. I . . .' But Red Goff appeared next to her before she could finish her sentence.

'Fenella? So you do know these Hamshomis?'

She turned to him and put her hand on his arm.

'Red, I think we'd better go round the back and talk.' She kept staring at Peter and me as if she couldn't believe her eyes. 'This way. There's a room at the back of the hall, behind the stage, where spare costumes are stored.'

She led us back through the small wooden door from which she had emerged, into a dingy room with benches round the walls. She gestured to us to sit down, then turned once more to her companion.

'They're not Hamshomis, Red. They're Black Star members from Earth.'

The dark-haired alien sat down.

'What? Are you serious? Earthlings? The oppressed themselves?'

'Fenella!' Peter was clearly shocked at our identity being revealed to someone who had spoken approvingly of brainwashing.

Red Goff was continuing to stare at us. 'I did wonder, when they tried out the old passwords on me,' he said, 'but then I thought it was just a Council trick. But if they're not the Hamshomis, then where are the real Hamshomis?'

'Waiting at the meeting point?' Fenella suggested gently.

'Oh . . .' Red Goff looked at her in dismay, and swore under his breath. 'The papers!'

'I think I'd better introduce you all before you dash off with those things again.' Fenella took Red Goff's arm and spoke to Peter and me. 'Red is the Black Star Gang's new leader. He is Ista Frith's son, BS Two. He's here on this planet because it's dangerous for him to be anywhere else.' She turned to Red Goff. 'Dominic and Peter are BS Eight and Nine, from Earth. I haven't the foggiest idea how they got here. I hope we're about to find out.'

I felt strangely sad and angry. Sad for Red Goff, because of what had happened to his mother, angry because Fenella was still hanging on to his arm.

'What are the new passwords?' I asked.

'What are these papers?' demanded Peter at the same time, holding on to the envelope in his pocket.

'The new passwords are "Hare Moon" and the reply is "silent" or "silence". Hare Moon is just an insignificant satellite of an insignificant planet in the Constellation Sagittarius, but we liked the name,' Fenella answered. 'You'll be surprised how easy it is to bring it into the conversation. As for the papers, they're very important for the welfare of this planet. Let's all go and deliver them together, shall we? Then we can talk on the way, and explain everything.'

We walked back through the city and on to the open heathland. The raw heat of the planet had lessened a little now and a slight breeze had arisen, quilting the air with ash. The sun was setting immoderately behind the volcanoes.

'The Hamshomis are sort of sweet, daft people, very

peaceable, who don't exactly help us but they don't hinder us either,' Fenella explained. 'I feel they've been showing signs of a willingness to do more, recently, but I may be wrong. They're a bit of a problem, actually, since we don't know how far we can trust them. They're sort of, ultra-responsible citizens, like, you know, inter-galactic senior prefects. They don't oppose the United Council of Planets. In fact most of them work for the Council in perfectly ordinary paid jobs. On the other hand a lot of them tend to write rather tight-lipped letters to the inter-planetary newspapers complaining about human rights infringements.'

Red Goff interrupted her.

'That's where they're different from us. We do something about it.'

Fenella nodded.

'The problem is that like any group of people, not all of them are quite so honest,' she continued. 'Some of them have been known to trade on their reputation for sweetness and naiveté, and have allowed themselves to be used by the Council to betray people whose trust they had gained. We believe this was how Ista Frith was taken.'

Red Goff turned his head away and stared into the distance, beyond the volcanoes.

Fenella glanced at him and bit her lip. 'At the moment they're acting as couriers between this planet, Bench Hellezine, and the United Council of Planets. They were the ideal people to do this simply because both sides will listen to them. Scientists here have come up with a plan to move Bench Hellezine's orbit further away from the sun, which would stop the quakes and volcanic eruptions, improve the climate all over the planet and allow things to grow.'

'It would also allow the computers to function better, which is the only reason the Council is even considering it,' put in Red Goff in a cynical voice. 'However, we'll meet that problem when we come to it.' He indicated Peter's pocket. 'What you have there are the detailed plans for the project.'

We had reached our red gravity-blaster.

'Oh.' Fenella stared at it, clearly overcome. 'I was going to ask you next how you got here, but now I know. How clever of you to find it, and how terribly clever of you to work out how to operate the trapdoor in the roof of the loft.'

Peter and I avoided each other's eyes.

'Tell me how things have been on Earth,' Fenella went on. We started to, but Red Goff interrupted.

'I must take the papers back to the meeting point. I can't risk the Hamshomis leaving without them.' Peter handed them over to him and the alien turned to go.

There was a shout in the distance. We all looked round, along the road that crossed the valley floor. A blue gravity-blaster with its roof open was skimming noiselessly along the dusty surface, raising a cloud behind it. Red Goff held tightly on to the papers, then as the craft reached us, visibly relaxed.

'Oh, welcome! My apologies for not meeting you. There was a misunderstanding. I've got the papers here. I hope you didn't wait out there too long . . .'

'No no, we were late ourselves. It was hardly any trouble at all,' said a slightly petulant voice as a very human looking alien with straight fair hair rose to his feet. 'Hardly any trouble at all, was it, Scupper?'

# Nine

'You would not *believe* what we went through to get here,' said Barty. He and Scupper were leaning against their gravity-blaster, staring around them at the hostile landscape with undisguised lack of enthusiasm. Scupper was black and had one gold earring. His long hair was tied back in a ponytail. 'How do you all *endure* to live here?' went on his friend. Peter opened his mouth, presumably to reply that we did not, but Fenella spoke quickly before he could.

'Oh, er, we tell ourselves that at least it's not as bad as Earth,' she replied lightly.

The two Hamshomis laughed and Scupper gave a whistle through his teeth.

'Dear me yes. I wish we didn't have to go back there, but unfortunately we do. They are *wild people* down there. We were sent to Earth by the Gravity-blaster Reclamation Department and first Barty lost his cat, then when our monitors picked up signals that a gravity-blaster was in the area, probably one left by those Black Star people, lo and behold the blessed thing exited through the roof before our very eyes. Roof tiles everywhere like an explosion in a cornflake factory, water tanks in the loft shattered, practically the whole house flooded. Poor Positron will never be the same again. He got really wet.' He stroked the cat, which had now settled itself on Barty's shoulder and was purring loudly.

'Oh. I see.' Fenella's voice was expressionless.

I met her eyes.

'Time we went, I think,' said Peter. I continued to look at Fenella in the diminishing light. Around our heads flakes of ash flew like roof tiles. The volcanoes on the darkening horizon glowed.

'Not yet,' I said. Apart from my reluctance to leave, I realised that we now had a major problem on our hands. If Barty and Scupper had to go back to Earth, how were we going to explain our presence there, living next door to the house demolished by a gravity-blaster? It would not take them very long to come to the right conclusion, and although they might be supportive towards the people of Bench Hellezine, I had no illusions that they would conspire to conceal the identity of Black Star members.

They must have been told by the Council, before going on their mission, that two Black Star members lived in the village of Stoke Stiley, and it had sounded from what we heard whilst hiding in the Old Rectory, that investigating them might even be part of their mission.

Barty looked at me enquiringly. 'Are you off somewhere too?' he asked. I wondered if here might lie the solution.

'Well yes, actually,' I replied hesitantly. 'In fact we have a mission on Earth too, but I'm afraid we can't talk about it.' I closed my lips and assumed a secretive expression.

Barty and Scupper nodded wisely.

'Oh yes, we understand, don't we, Scupper.'

'Indeed we do. Well, the best of luck with it. Maybe we'll meet up, while you're there.' Scupper gave a friendly grin. 'Goodbye then. Come on Barty. Let's get these papers delivered. It may do no good. You know that, don't you.' He spoke to Red Goff. 'Old Benet Rogery, the only scientist who can do the orbit-shift, is out of favour with the powers that be, just now. Anyway, we'll do our best.'

The two Hamshomis climbed back into their blue gravity-blaster.

'Good luck!' called Fenella. We all waved as they took off. When they were gone she turned and hugged Peter and then me. 'You idiots. You could have killed yourselves, going through the roof like that. We ought to check this gravity-blaster before you fly off in it again. Did it seem to be functioning all right?'

I nodded. 'I'm really sorry about the house, Fenella. Yes, the gravity-blaster seemed fine. Newt stopped functioning properly as we neared this planet, but he had warned us in advance about that.'

'Oh, dear old Newt!' She advanced on the gravity-blaster and stared in through the glass dome. 'Will you reprogram him with the new passwords when he starts functioning again, please?'

I nodded once more. Red Goff was walking round the spacecraft, peering at it critically. 'This thing really ought to be checked out before you leave,' he said. 'They're not indestructible, you know.'

Peter shook his head.

'Look, I'm sorry, but there's no time. We've been away an awfully long time already. My mum will be going mad. I'm supposed to be babysitting for my cousin at four o'clock.' He opened the glass dome and climbed in. 'Come on, Dominic. We can come back tomorrow.'

I looked at Fenella in despair. Red Goff had put his arm around her.

'All right. We'll be back tomorrow,' I said. 'Where will you be?'

'In the rooms over the hall where the rock concert was held.'

'About the same time?'

'Well, our time will be different from your time because we turn faster, but I'll stay in until you arrive.'

It didn't make up for Red Goff's arm around her, but it was better than nothing. I turned to get into the gravity-blaster. It was nearly dark now. My own arm was still rather painful, but not as painful as seeing Fenella's excessive friendliness towards this stranger.

'What happened to Mitzalie and Claude?' I asked almost as an afterthought, realising that the other Black Star members who had been our friends on Earth had not been mentioned. Fenella shook her head and looked away. Red Goff answered for her, his voice flat.

'Council guards got them.' He raised his hand in a gesture of farewell. 'Go safely. Have a good flight. We'll see you tomorrow.' He and Fenella turned away as I joined Peter in the gravity-blaster and closed the glass dome over our heads.

# Ten

Newt did not start to respond to my input until we had gone beyond hypervortex and were well away from Bench Hellezine. Peter programmed him with the passwords 'Hare Moon' and 'silence' and the computer thanked us politely and said he had preferred the old ones. Then he tipped sideways.

At first I could not comprehend what had happened. There was a crash, and Peter, who had omitted to fasten his safety belt, fell out of his seat. Then I saw that the entire front control console and computer section of the spacecraft had come loose, and had slid with its considerable weight into Peter's seat, catapulting him sideways.

'Peter!' I unclipped my own belt and moved to help my friend, then stopped. Something was flickering on the control panel. There was a light inside it, behind the keys. I stared, and leaned closer.

'Newt?' I checked that the voice control was on.

'Newt, there's a light flickering in the keyboard. What is it?'

The computer did not reply. A fear grew in my chest. Peter lay motionless against the side of the gravity-blaster, vibrating with its movement. We seemed to be going faster.

'Newt!' I spoke sharply and loudly. 'Planet Earth's co-ordinates, please! I want you to get us there very very fast. Do you hear me?'

There was a squeak from the machine. I hammered the voice control button. It was hot. 'Newt! This is Dominic. The password is Hare Moon. Or the old one if you prefer it. I believe we met aboard the Starship Ashkey.'

For a moment there was still no reply. The stars were sweeping towards and past us. They looked like snow in a car's headlights on a winter night, or like ash on an alien planet. They were hypnotic, and for a moment I felt I could have gone on like this for ever to see what lay at the edge of the universe.

I dragged my attention away from this treacherous notion and stared at the controls. Was there some sort of override? I could not remember. I glanced again at Peter. I must help him, but first I must program some sense into Newt and stop what was becoming an increasingly mindless hurtle into deep space.

I worked at the lopsided controls and they burnt my fingers. The stars streamed by faster. It was difficult to remember instructions when a headlong topple into eternity was going on outside the window. There was a hiss from the keyboard. The flicker brightened. A small flame snaked up past one of the keys. I looked at it. I was in deep space and there was a flame on my control panel.

'Rabbits,' said the computer.

My head jerked up and I stared at the machine. Rabbits? I must have misheard.

'Planet Earth's co-ordinates, please,' I repeated in a shaky voice, feeling insane with relief that it was responding. My hand was poised over the keyboard to tap in the vital digits which would take us home.

'Rabbits, rabbits.' Newt's normal voice sounded distorted. 'Rabbits, rabbits,' it repeated, its voice sinking to a hollow boom. 'Rabbits. There is a malfunction. I am a malfunctioning rabbit. I am . . . a . . . dear, little . . . malfunctioning . . . rabb . . .' The voice faded away.

'Newt! Newt! You are not a rabbit! Newt! You must give me Planet Earth's co-ordinates. Forget Hare Moon. Forget rabbits. There's something wrong with our controls and we're going too fast! We're on fire!' As if it had heard me the flame spiralled out from the keyboard again and acrid fumes leaked into the cabin. Newt's voice sounded again, low and deep, as if he were a giant.

'I am checking all information on small furry rodents and will supply the information you require as soon as possible.' Then he fell silent.

I sat quite still for a moment whilst the full situation dawned on me, then I put out an emergency help call on both the gravity-blaster's communicator and the Black Star communicator which was in my ear. There was no reply on either. At the speed we had been going I realised we might easily be out of range of all populated planets. I called again, but there was only silence.

I clambered over to where Peter lay and lifted him carefully to assess his injuries. He flopped against me, eyes closed, a puppet with cloth limbs.

Briefly I switched off the gravity – that at least was working – and floated him back into his seat. A Tom-and-Jerry bump was growing on the side of his head, but he was breathing and his heart was beating regularly. I sat him in his seat, strapped him in and turned back to the controls. The flame had disappeared now but I had to sit back from the controls because of the heat.

At least, perhaps, I could try and deal with this excessive speed at which we were travelling, then I would try and find a fire extinguisher. At the moment the fire was inaccessible behind the control panel. I pulled the control unit back into position before switching the gravity back on. I put my foot on the reverse thrust. It gave way loosely, exerting no resistance and no braking power.

Feeling sick, I next pulled at the manual backup lever which was in the wall. There was a crack, and it came away in my hand. With a sudden lunge the tiny vehicle tipped completely on to its side. There was a shriek in my ears and the stars accelerated into a blur. Hanging on my side, slowly sliding out of my seatbelt, with

Peter lolling grotesquely above me, I hit every key I could find then, reserve power, emergency backup braking and every co-ordinate on the console. Any planet would be better than none.

Nothing happened.

At that moment Peter slithered out of his seatbelt and fell on top of me. I was crushed against the glass dome, my own seatbelt biting painfully into my side. I struggled to reach the gravity button to float him off, but when I did manage to reach it, it was too hot to touch.

That was when I saw what looked like a strange sunrise above my head. For a moment my brain could not work it out. Daylight? Morning? I struggled to push Peter to one side so that I could see past him. He was a dead weight. The whites of his eyes were flickering horribly between his eyelids. His head bounced painfully against mine.

At last I managed to lever him away, and then I saw that above my head, in the space between the two layers of the glass dome, great bright flames were leaping.

# Eleven

Almost at once the heat became unbearable and the fumes suffocating. Terror gave me strength. I hauled myself to the small storage cupboards behind the seats and tore them open. Did scoot-suits work in space? Now seemed like a good time to find out. Sweat poured off me and the fumes began to choke me. I put my Black Star communicator on open channel and just left it to transmit the coughing and wheezing that was coming from my chest.

There were space suits in one of the little cupboards. I dragged one out and started to cram Peter into it. It was like trying to dress an unco-operative baby in a large Babygro. The heat and smoke, and the juddering of the spacecraft, hindered me. I began coughing uncontrollably. I realised that one of Peter's hands in the space suit sleeve was bent back at the wrist and had not gone into the glove. There was nothing I could do about that now. There was no time.

I pulled up the zip fastener and caught his chin in it,

drawing blood. I winced for him. In a brief moment of elation I saw that the space suits had little scoot-suit engines on their backs and control switches in the palms of their gloves. That at least was one complication fewer.

At last Peter was safely in the suit with his helmet screwed on top. He's got his head screwed on right, I heard Auntie's voice in my head, and I wondered if the fumes were turning my brain.

Now I must get into a space suit myself. I felt dizzy. It was almost impossible to see across the cabin and there was a thick smell of incinerating plastic. I shook out the other suit and started to climb into it fast. Hot chemical breath touched me on the cheek like the halitosis of an unkempt friend. I felt too exhausted suddenly to fumble with the zip. My hands were too clumsy in the gloves to put the helmet on.

There was a crack behind me. I looked over my shoulder. The control panel was buckling. Keys crumpled like polystyrene. But now my helmet was on. Searing fumes were trapped inside it with my head but they cleared instantly. At once it was intensely cool in the suit and the sweat dried in cold flakes all over my body.

I hauled Peter up against my shoulder, grabbed the small fire extinguisher from its clip on the wall and reached for the catch to release the glass dome. I needed a rope to fasten us together, but there was no time and I could not see for the smoke. The fire was too close and too dangerous now. I must fight it from outside.

For one brief nightmare moment I wondered if the dome might not open. In that same moment the fire turned into a wall of flame and came roaring at me across the cabin. I looked oblivion in the face, then the dome was open, the gravity-blaster zig-zagged wildly and Peter and I were tipped into space.

It was cold, blissfully cold, in space. We hurtled away from the gravity-blaster for a few moments with the impetus of our exit, then slowed to a gentle, orbiting roll.

I looked back. The fire in the cabin had gone out, without air to fuel it, but from within the sealed undersection of the spacecraft the glow and flash of flames still showed. I must get back and try to put that out. The entire interior of the gravity-blaster looked warped and blackened, and the control panel had either melted or fallen out when we did. I suppose I knew then that it was hopeless, but the alternative, to be lost in space without shelter, did not bear contemplation.

I tried out the scoot-suit controls in my palm. The little engine pushed like a firm hand on my back. I linked my arm round Peter's – if only I had a rope – and grappled with the fire extinguisher under my other arm as we moved back in the direction of the gravity-blaster. Then I looked down.

There is no up or down in space. I knew that then and

I know it now. You can't fall because there's no gravity, and there's no gravity because there's no planetary body beneath to pull you. There's nothing. Nothing beneath your feet at all, for miles and miles.

Try and imagine that moment. Be with me in that moment, because I was more alone then than I have ever been. Even if there are just your imaginations there with me, intangible and hopelessly too late, it is better than nothing. Night after night I live it again in my sleep, and every time it is as real as it ever was.

In the long moment that I hung there, frozen, the gravity-blaster began to jerk erratically to and fro. Then it started to spiral away. In horror I clenched my hand on the scoot-suit button and tried to pursue it, but it was moving too quickly, accelerating into a catherine wheel of light.

At last, despairing, I released my scoot-suit controls and hung motionless, watching it go. It was a little miracle of alien invention, our contact with Earth and our transport home, and now, just another tiny point of light in the universe.

I realised I was holding Peter's arm too tightly. My own injured arm ached and throbbed. My hand had gone numb. I was feeling very cold. I wondered how one regulated the temperature in these space suits. I discovered a sliding button in the sleeve and turned up the heat for both of us.

Peter was still unconscious. His red crewcut looked terribly vulnerable in the blackness of space. I used the power from my scoot-suit to turn us both slowly in a full circle. I could see nothing, in the whole universe, to help us.

After hanging there for what seemed like a long time, I decided to move towards the brightest star I could see. I knew that there was almost certainly no point in this, because without hypervortex travel we stood no chance of reaching either a planet or a space station. However, there was nothing else to do.

'BS Eight to Black Star Gang,' I said softly inside my helmet. 'Black Star Gang? Is anyone out there?'

There was no reply.

We moved through space for a long time. Every so often I rearranged Peter, my hands gripping clumsily at the folds of his space suit. I dared not let go of him even for a moment. I was afraid that he might drift off and that I would not be able to catch him again.

'Peter, wake up.' I spoke to him occasionally, but it was more for my own benefit than for his. I felt he was probably better off unconscious. I wondered whether, if we travelled through space for the whole of time, we would ever meet another human being. Perhaps some future interstellar mission, powered by Mr Batworthy's hypo-relativity discovery which had got us into such trouble with the aliens in the first place, would pass this way. Hello, do you come here often? Sorry I'm a skeleton.

How long did it take to go mad in space? I wondered

which would come first, madness, starvation or suffocation. Now *there* was a thought. How much oxygen did I have? I glanced over my shoulder at the slight hunchback effect that was my compressed oxygen pack, then I looked at the gauge on my sleeve. It seemed to be registering half full. What did half full mean in terms of survival time? I had no idea.

Pains started to come and go in my hands. We travelled on and on. It felt as though weeks had passed. What day was it? Of course there were no days out here, just eternity. What day had it been when I left Earth? I could not remember. Did I shine, I wondered, like a star?

My arm went numb. I towed Peter by his arm, his leg, his head. I pushed him along in front of me. Space was really boring. All of you out there who think space is fascinating, forget it. It is really boring.

I began to experience pains in my stomach, and to feel sleepy. I jolted myself awake. To be sleepy was to be dead. The bright star that was my goal looked no nearer, but then it wasn't, in practical terms. The amount by which I had moved towards it would be too tiny to show up in any mathematical equation, no matter how complex, nor would it ever show up, even if I travelled for the whole of my lifetime.

That was why Mr Batworthy's hypo-relativity discovery was of such importance. It would enable those of us on Earth to travel among the stars in quite manageable periods of time. It was the reason that our computer teacher was now on the run, hunted by aliens who wanted to wipe his brain clear as they had done to his American counterpart.

I thought of the last words which the Black Star Gang's leader, BS One, had said to me before she herself was captured. 'Find Batworthy.' I knew that there must still be more to discover, but now I never should.

Sleep rocked me and slackened my hands. I grasped at Peter in panic, slapping my free hand against my leg to stay awake. I began gnashing my teeth together loudly to snap my brain into alertness.

I remembered suddenly a long gone lesson in the school computer room, with the sun coming in through the window. I had felt drowsy then and had tried surreptitiously clacking my teeth together to stay awake. I remembered Mr Batworthy saying, 'That's odd. What do we have here?' and I had thought he was referring to me. Then, at our enquiring expressions, 'Oh, oh nothing my dears. Computers are full of surprises.'

My eyes closed. I forced them open and started to talk to myself. 'Computers are full of surprises,' I said. What, in our school computer, had so surprised Mr Batworthy?

I dreamed. The windows of the computer room were open. Bright sunshine patterned the floor. Outside the window, insects buzzed and crackled in the long grass at the edge of the playing field. I sat drowsily in the dust motes and watched Mr Batworthy pushing his hands through his untidy grey hair, making it stand on end, an expression of astonishment on his face. He scribbled a lot of very fast calculations on an upturned tissue box then turned back to his screen. 'Well, well,' he said. 'Well, well.'

When I woke, the sound of insects buzzing and crackling was in my head, and Peter had gone.

# Twelve

I haven't cried very often in recent years, but I did then.

'Peter!' I shouted. 'Peter!' If his communicator, deep in his ear channel, was working, perhaps he would hear me through his unconsciousness.

It was not my Black Star communicator that answered me though. Instead, a voice sounded in my space helmet, echoing round my head.

'It's all right,' it said. 'We have your friend. Keep talking. You're too small to show up on our monitors and we need to use your voice as a homing device.'

'Hello?' My voice was a baffled squeak. 'Hello?'

'Hello, Dominic.' It was Peter. He sounded as though he had difficulty in speaking, his voice thick and fuddled.

'Keep talking, Dominic,' repeated the other voice. 'You need to keep talking. Say anything.'

'Hello,' I said. 'I don't know what to say. Hello hello hello.' I realised that I was feeling very ill.

'Recite something,' Peter commanded. He sounded anxious. 'Recite "Mary had a little lamb".'

Wondering blackly if Peter was suffering from even worse oxygen deficiency than I was, I tried. 'Mary had a little ham, ramble, ram, rabbit . . .' I felt confused and faint. The buzzing and crackling in my ears had increased and now my chest hurt. I tried once more to speak, but my tongue felt fat and huge, like a massive piece of meat one had accidentally bitten off and was too polite to spit out.

'Mary had a little bat . . .' I couldn't breathe. I really couldn't breathe now. 'Help!' I tried to call. It came out in a gurgle and my limbs started to jerk uncontrollably. The stars turned into coloured lights flashing across my eyes. As I attempted to inhale, a pain like an axe blow crashed into my chest.

Then, among the coloured lights, there was a solid dot, the size of a pinprick. It was moving fast towards me and it was blue, blue like Earth.


I was five. I was in Taunton's Musgrove Park Hospital, in an oxygen tent. The concerned faces of nurses and my parents were peering at me through the transparent plastic. Bright lights glared overhead.

'Mum?' I held out my arms to my mother and I saw that she was fighting back tears.

'Here's Beamish.' She held my old teddy bear against the outside of the plastic tent. 'He'll sit with me and wait until you're better.'

I could feel the asthma attack easing off. I closed my eyes and breathing became easier. The lights dimmed and I could hear my mother's breathing too, a smooth susurrus against the rasping of my own. There was a thump. Beamish must have fallen on to the floor. Cautiously, enjoying the pleasure of breathing, I opened my eyes.

'Your friend's coming round, Peter,' said a voice. A pale face with floppy hair peered at me. 'Hello Dominic,' said Barty. He turned his head and I saw Peter beyond him. 'There shouldn't be any brain damage. His oxygen had only just run out,' added the alien. 'Would you shut the inner dome, please?'

The same thump I had just heard came again. Then Peter's face loomed over mine.

'Hi.' He looked shocked. His face was puffy and white.

'Hi.' I tried to smile, gave up, closed my eyes and slept.

I can't have slept for much more than an hour, but when I woke, Earth was visible through the glass dome of the spacecraft and I felt remarkably well. Even the lingering pain in my left arm had gone. I found that I was curled into the small space at the back of a gravity-blaster, next to the storage cupboards, and that I was covered with a mound of soft, light blankets. On top of the blankets slept the beeping cat, its face close to mine. It was purring. Scupper was kneeling next to me. He smiled and peeled something off my forehead.

'I gave you a dose of general panacea. Feeling better?'

I nodded, and raised myself on one elbow. Barty and Peter, who were sitting in the front, both turned to look at me. I saw that Peter, too, looked much more his normal self.

'Well, what a nightmare you two have been through!' exclaimed Barty. 'Welcome back to the land of the living. It was a stroke of amazing luck for you that Bench Hellezine's magnetic field seems to have accidentally scrambled the computer sensors of our two spacecraft. It must have happened when we were both parked outside the city of Stot. We couldn't understand what was happening at first, when our screen started clocking grossly hyper-photic speeds when we were travelling as normal at just a few times the speed of light. Then when our computer started relaying your emergency call, we understood what must have occurred. I'm sorry it took us so long to reach you, but you really had travelled rather a long way.'

Scupper was still looking at me with concern. 'Are you both sure you're fit to go on with your mission?' he asked. 'Peter assures me you are, but we can just as easily turn round again and take you back home, can't we, Barty, or drop you off for some recuperative brain-processing at the Alpha Centauri Interchange.'

I shook my head emphatically.

'Er, no thanks.'

'I'm sure you could do with a couple of days' leave,' added Scupper. 'From what I've heard the Earth project isn't *that* urgent.'

Earth project? Suddenly I remembered Scupper's and Barty's knowing look when I had said, back on Bench Hellezine, that we were involved with something on Earth that we could not discuss. I felt myself turning cold, despite the blankets.

'Oh well, I suppose you want setting down at Stoke Stiley then, do you?' Barty enquired.

'Ye-e-es,' said Peter slowly, glancing at me. 'Stoke Stiley would be a good place to put us down.'

'We might see you around. We'll be working in that area too.' The alien operated the controls on manual. 'We have a really brilliant cover,' he added. 'It was that dreadful woman Commander Parry's idea. She said she'd done something similar during the first Earth Project, but it does seem the perfect excuse for going round knocking on people's doors . . .'

He stopped speaking as the small spacecraft juddered with the braking effect of entering Earth's atmosphere. Clouds fogged the glass dome for a moment. Then our village was below us, clusters of small houses I had thought never to see again, the school I had dreamt of whilst lost in space, all of them golden in the sunlight of a summer evening.

# Thirteen

They set us down in the woods behind the school. With its invisibility screen on, we were unable to see the gravity-blaster once we had stepped out of it, but we heard Scupper's voice call out, 'Good luck!'

Peter and I arranged to meet early the next morning. We were both too tired and shaken by the day's events to talk now. We parted and went home. I felt as if I had been away far longer than a day. I endured Granny Probity's wrath at my unexplained absence, ate three fried egg sandwiches and went to bed.

I slept deeply. I had no idea what time it was when the noise woke me. It stopped as I struggled into wakefulness. I listened, tense, in the total darkness. The sound came again, a scratching from over by the window. I turned over to face it, pausing as my bedsprings creaked, turning further until I could see the red digits of my alarm clock. It was two o'clock.

The noise came again. It was louder this time, a rough scrabbling. I wondered if we had mice. The night was hot. Cautiously I pushed the quilt back and eased myself up on to one elbow.

This time I knew it could not be mice. Mice could not unlatch windows. All my bedroom windows were partly open because of the heat, and the sound I could hear now was the click of one of the notched arms which held the window steady, as someone reached in and raised it. For a moment I was rigid with indecision, then I hurled myself out of bed and flung back the curtains.

There was a gasp. A dark figure lurched backwards. Instinctively I reached out and grabbed it as it teetered on a dimly glimpsed ladder. It gave a whimper, and for a moment I could hardly hold it, then I braced myself and hauled it in over the windowsill. It fell to the floor, clumsy and moaning.

I suppose I had hoped it was Fenella. One does hope these things in the middle of the night, doesn't one, unlikely as they might seem. They don't happen though, do they, and they didn't happen then. I switched on my bedside light and saw that it was Mr Batworthy.

I was almost too astonished to speak. 'Mr Batworthy . . . how . . . ?'

He was struggling to his feet. He shook his head and sank into my cane chair. He looked frail and thin and much older than when I had last seen him. He appeared to be clad in rags. His face and hands were filthy. He looked nothing at all like the easy-going scientist who had taught computer studies at Stoke Stiley school so recently, and who had also discovered how to travel faster than light.

He must have seen my expression because he smiled tightly. It looked painful.

'I've walked from Lancashire, Dominic,' he said. 'I've had to travel by night and hide by day. The aliens are out to destroy my brain.'

I sat on the bed near him. He sagged. His chin slumped on to his chest. I reached for a pillow and put it behind his head.

'You look terrible, sir. What can I do for you first? Do you want something to eat?'

He nodded. 'Water first, Dominic, then food. Then . . .'

'Then sleep, from the look of you,' I interrupted. 'You can scarcely even sit. I'll hide you. Don't worry.'

'No.' He shook his head. 'No, Dominic. I have to get into the school . . .'

'The school?' I was astounded. This seemed like the last place for him to go, since the aliens would look for him there first if they realised he was in the area.

'No . . . I must.' He could hardly speak.

I went quickly out of the room and brought him a glass of water from the bathroom. He downed it almost in one swallow, the liquid slopping out of the corners of his mouth and down his chin.

'More, I'll get you more, Mr Batworthy.'

'No!' He held out his hand to stop me. 'Dominic, you

have to know this. One more person has to know this. I'm sorry if it endangers you but . . .' He began choking. I supported his shoulders until he stopped, then I fetched him more water. He took it impatiently and drank it, then continued speaking almost without pause.

'I was pushing the main school computer to its limits one day, Dominic, playing with it I suppose, during a lesson one hot sunny day when none of you seemed able to concentrate. Really I was just seeing what it could do. Dominic, I accidentally keyed into something else. I think it was another computer, or some sort of adjunct to ours.' He looked at me as if unsure whether to go on.

'It contained strange symbols, like hieroglyphics, and extraordinarily long and complicated equations and formulae . . .' He was becoming short of breath. He clutched his chest.

'You need a doctor, Mr Batworthy. I'd better get a doctor. Doctor Ruth from round the corner will come. She won't give you away.'

'No!' He almost shouted it. 'Let me finish! Don't you see, Dominic? It's something the aliens put there. The aliens have added something to the school computer and we don't know what it is. It could be anything. It could be some sort of self-destruct mechanism which might blow the world up. We don't know. We have to find out. I have to get into the school and find out. They captured me before I could go much further with it last time, and I'm sure they don't know what I've seen.' He heaved himself to his feet and swayed.

'All right. All right, we'll go to the school, but first you're going to have some food.' I walked out of the room before he could argue with me, and went downstairs to the kitchen. Everything was in the wrong place. Granny Probity had been clearing up again. I searched until I found a tin of baked beans and the bread, then made my teacher baked beans on toast and a cup of strong coffee.

Was one supposed to give people coffee if they seemed to be on the verge of a heart attack? I wasn't sure. I made myself a cup too. I felt dizzy with tiredness and a sense of unreality. Alien hieroglyphics in the school computer? Could this be part of the reason why the aliens had had to refrain from blowing us all up back in April? Could this, conceivably, be the thing that they hadn't had time to relocate?

If so, what was it?

I went back upstairs with the tray of food and drink. Mr Batworthy appeared to have fallen asleep. I left him for a few moments and drank my coffee. I felt desperately that I needed to talk to someone who knew more than I did about the United Council of Planets and their business. I needed to talk to Fenella, even more than I normally needed to talk to Fenella.

I thought about Red Goff, with his taut, brittle manner and perceptive stare. I thought about Claude and Mitzalie, our old friends in the Black Star Gang, now presumably brain-processed zombies. I felt very alone.

Mr Batworthy woke up.

'There's something else I have to do,' he said. I passed him his food. 'Thank you. If I get into the school I can retrieve my work on the hypo-relativity syndrome and publish it. Then there will be no point in the aliens wiping my brain, if all the other time scientists in the world know the secret.'

I nodded. This made sense. 'But do you honestly think your papers will still be there, sir?' I asked. 'The aliens will have gone through everything.'

My teacher smiled slightly. A baked bean adhered to his chin. He nodded. 'Oh yes, Dominic, the work will still be there. I'm fairly sure of that.'

# Fourteen

I was thankful for once that both Auntie and Granny Probity were slightly deaf, for we seemed to make an awful lot of noise getting out of the house. It was still completely dark in the lane. I walked carefully and surely, but Mr Batworthy, unfamiliar with the potholes, kept stumbling. I did not dare to switch on the torch I had brought, in case some local insomniac saw us.

We entered the school grounds by the side gate and walked across the playground.

'How are we going to get into the building?' I whispered.

Mr Batworthy felt in his pocket and produced a key. 'The usual way,' he grinned.

It was strange to be in the school at night. I risked switching on the torch as we walked down the main corridor. In the computer room I went round all the windows drawing down the blinds. Mr Batworthy moved to the side area which housed the main frame computer.

'I'll need a few minutes,' he said.

I watched his fingers moving rapidly over the keys. He had the same rapport with the machine that I had noticed in Fenella. There was something about these people who had an affinity with computers, a sort of second nature that linked them to machines in an instinctive partnership, that was unsettling. I think it was because it made the machines, in their turn, seem more human, less like subservient technology and more like something animate.

I watched Mr Batworthy for a few moments more, then paced round the room, willing him to hurry up, hearing with increased tension the tiny night noises of the school.

After several minutes my teacher glanced over his shoulder at me, as if in irritation.

'Dominic, you can go and get the hypo-relativity syndrome for me while you're waiting.'

'What? Where is it?'

'In the playground.'

'In the playground?' I repeated his words stupidly. My mind struggled to imagine where in the playground a scientist could have hidden the most important discovery of the century. I had imagined it under lock and key, in a safe.

'You'll need your torch and a piece of paper.'

I picked up my torch and took a sheet of A4 from the top of the filing cabinet. 'Yes?'

Of course! Understanding dawned. He must have buried it. How clever of him. 'Will I need a spade, sir?'

Mr Batworthy shook his head and frowned, concentrating, still rattling away at the keys.

'If I could just remember exactly what I did . . . No Dominic. You won't need a spade. You know the bike shed?'

I did.

'You know the headmaster's policy of allowing graffiti on the bike shed?'

'Yes.' This was a cause of dissent among some parents who foolishly strayed down that end of the playground. They were upset by some of the messages and drawings which appeared in multicoloured spray-paint and ink. The headmaster said that he was only upset if the messages were misspelt.

His argument was that if the students weren't allowed to express themselves there, they would express themselves on the walls of the school itself. He was probably right, but the general feeling among students was that some of the fun had gone out of it now that it was permitted.

'Go and look at the wall that faces down towards the canal,' went on Mr Batworthy, 'and copy down everything on that wall, exactly as it appears.'

I lowered myself into one of the desk chairs.

'You mean . . . ?'

'Yes, it's a coded version of the hypo-relativity formula, with additional references to the left luggage lockers round the county where my papers and the record of my research are hidden. You must copy it down *exactly*, with the same spacing and comparative letter sizes. Can you do that?'

'Yes . . . yes sir, I can.'

'You'll need your torch. It should be safe enough to use it down there. Go on now. I need to concentrate.'

I went.

Down at the bike shed I stood and looked at the closely worked tapestry of graffiti that covered all sides. 'Dominic loves Louise.' That was an old one.

Some were wittier than others. Beneath 'Mr Wadhams is a weirdo' was 'Dyslexia rules – KO'. I walked round to the far side. This side was the fullest. I stared at it in dismay. This was going to take some time.

By the time I returned to the school, two hours had passed and the sky was lightening in the east. I went in quietly by the side door. The blinds were still down in the computer room. I opened the door.

'I've got it sir . . .' I stopped. Mr Batworthy was standing up, his hands clasped to his chest.

'Look! Look! I've got it back! I've gone through the secret link! What is it? Tell me now, boy, what is it?'

I rushed over to the machine and as I reached it I felt a wave of fright wash over me. The screen was covered minutely with the fine hieroglyphics of the interplanetary language.

I looked at it for a long time. It was a strange experience to see this writing here. The last time I had

81

seen it was on Newt's screen, giving me information about the planet Bench Hellezine. For a moment I thought I must suddenly have lost my ability to read it. Then I realised. This was some sort of code.

'What does it say? Do you understand it?' shouted my teacher. 'You understand their language, don't you? Is that what it is? What does it say?'

I sat down and stared closely at the screen. There were graphs, formulae and equations, but the actual language that accompanied them was completely incomprehensible.

I shook my head.

'I don't know what it says. It *is* the interplanetary language, or at least the symbols are the same, but it seems to be some sort of code. Scroll it on a bit and let's see what comes next.'

None of it was any better. There were pages and pages of the stuff. After an hour we gave up.

'I'll tell you what,' I muttered. 'Let's just print this out on the freewriter and I'll take it away with me. Peter's very good with codes, and he could work on it, but there are some people on another planet I can ask, too. They might really know what it all means.' I thought of Fenella and Red Goff. 'I'm going up there today.'

Mr Batworthy stared at me.

'You mean you're still involved in all this, Dominic? After what nearly happened to you last time?' He swivelled his chair so that he faced me. 'Don't! It's not worth it, boy. They've gone, haven't they? Nothing is worth the risks you'd be taking.'

I relived, for a blank, terrified moment, the blazing gravity-blaster, being lost in space, the utter helplessness of suffocation. Was it worth it? No, never.

He was still watching me closely.

'They *have* gone, haven't they? They won't even bother coming after me once I publish the hypo-relativity syndrome and it's too late for them to do anything about it.' He propped his fingers together and leaned back in his chair, tucking his chin into his neck. I paused. With the back of my hand I wiped the sweat from my forehead.

'No, Mr Batworthy. No, they had gone, but they're back. They're here now, two of them. I'm not quite sure why, yet. What I do know is that more of them are coming, and I think it must be something to do with what you've discovered here. One of them implied to me, not knowing who I was, that the new project was centred on Stoke Stiley. Whatever it is, it must be connected with their plans for Earth, and one thing I do know. They only mean us harm.'

My teacher shook his head. 'They didn't blow us up last time, but you think they may still mean to?'

I thought for a moment, gazing in despair at the meaningless jumble of symbols, signs and pictograms.

'You see, sir, you may have been the only reason they didn't destroy us last time. The leader of the Black Star Gang said something about them needing to relocate someone or something first. It could be that they want to be sure your information is wiped out and your brain blanked before they risk any sort of final chaos in which you could escape. The two aliens could be here to capture you, and this . . .' I gestured at the screenful of gibberish. 'This could be the means of activating something at long range. It could be set already. It could be . . . a time bomb.'

# Fifteen

It was clear that Mr Batworthy's safety must be one of my prime concerns. Between us we decided that he should hide at the school, in a storeroom in the vast basement, where he would be less likely to be found by any searching aliens. I would bring bedding and food for him.

I switched over to the freewriter and started printing out the coded words and diagrams. The machine gently hissed out sheets of paper as daylight started to shine round the blinds.

'I'll see what Peter can make of these and I'll show them to my other friends too. I'll bring you food and a couple of blankets later.' I put the sheets of paper into a cardboard folder. Before I left I carried a mattress from Matron's room down to the basement. At the last moment I remembered the paper on which I had so laboriously reproduced the graffiti from the bike shed.

'Oh,' I said hesitantly, 'there's this.'

Mr Batworthy took it from me and scanned it superficially.

'Good gracious, they have added a lot. Never mind. I know which are mine.' He frowned. 'Dear me, I think we could have done without this.'

I looked over his shoulder.

'Oh, er, yes. I wasn't sure about including that one, sir.'

'No no, you had to.' He laughed shortly. 'I wanted everything.'

'Kindness to animals – Mr Batworthy's hairdo should be released into the wild', said the message. I gave a sympathetic shrug.

'Try and get some rest. I'll be back this evening.'

On the way home it hit me – everything, the escape through the roof, finding Fenella, the fire in the gravity-blaster, and now the night spent in the school.

My knees began to wobble. I held on to the fence which imprisoned Peter's goat at the top end of Home Meadow. The animal rushed up on its long chain and slammed into the wooden fence post, as was its habit. I had been terrified of this animal when I was a child. Now it was quite amusing to see how close one could stand without being butted or chewed at by it. It raised its head and gave me its usual brain-dead amber stare, then backed away and began eating a crisp packet.

I watched it for a few minutes while the strength returned to my legs. My hand on the fence post surprised me by trembling uncontrollably. I clenched and unclenched it a few times until it stopped. It occurred to me that what I needed was sleep. Was there time for a couple of hours? I looked down at the sheets of paper in my hand, with their rows and rows of incomprehensible symbols, and realised that no, there was no time for sleeping.

When I arrived home, Auntie and Granny Probity were watching breakfast television. Granny Probity was standing in the middle of the living room with her arms raised, concentrating on 'Fitness with Fatima'. On the television screen a sleek Asian girl in a camouflage patterned leotard and combat boots was standing in the same position as Granny Probity. There the resemblance ended.

'Arms *raise* and bend, stretch!' shouted the girl.

Granny Probity bent and stretched in her floppy pink dressing gown, her face rapidly becoming a similar shade of pink. 'Come on Veronica,' she puffed at Auntie. 'Join in. This is good for you.'

Auntie shuddered and sank deeper into her chair with her cup of black coffee.

'And *swing*!' commanded Fatima. I ducked as Granny Probity's arms whirled. I went and sat down next to Auntie.

'Hi Auntie,' I said.

'Hello lad.' Auntie beamed. 'You're out of bed early. I haven't seen much of you lately. What have you been up to?'

'Oh, getting around, you know. I saw Fenella Brown. Do you remember her?'

'Gracious me, how could I forget her? I thought your dad said you weren't to have any more to do with aliens.'

'She's got a new boyfriend.'

Auntie's face crumpled with sympathy. 'That's a real bummer, lad. Still, she wasn't exactly your girlfriend, was she?'

I reflected for a moment. 'No, I suppose she wasn't, exactly.' But she would have been, I added silently to myself, and realised how much my view of Fenella had changed over the past few months.

Granny Probity was now raising her knees and stretching out her feet rhythmically to some powerful rock music. One of her slippers flew off and hit the far wall.

'Lord preserve her. She's going to kill herself,' muttered Auntie. She turned back to me. 'You missed the explosion, lad.'

'Explosion? What do you mean, Auntie?'

'Next door. It blew up yesterday. I forgot to tell you when you got home last night because I was right cross with you for being out so long. They reckon it was the gas. Fair shook the neighbourhood it did. That's what you get when you leave a nice house like that standing empty for so long. Blows up, it does. There's plenty of folks would be glad to live in a house like that instead of on the streets.' She shook her head. 'Coffee, lad?'

I nodded. 'Thanks.' My eyelids were closing. I needed something to keep me awake.

I felt amused and relieved that our exit through the roof had been interpreted as a gas explosion.

Auntie eased herself out of her chair and headed for the kitchen. The doorbell rang.

'That'll be the milkman,' panted Granny Probity. 'I asked him for a dozen live yoghurts and I don't suppose he's got them.'

'I'll go.' Auntie's footsteps changed direction in the hall. A few moments later she returned to the living room looking puzzled.

'It's an Irishman,' she said. 'Says his name's Paddy O'Dawes. I can't make out what he wants. You'd better talk to him, Probity.'

Curious, I followed Granny Probity into the hall. Her large bulk filled the doorway.

'Paddy O'Dawes? Yes, what can I do for you, young man? Are you the milkman?'

'Er, no.' The voice sounded familiar. I stepped forward, sure that I knew this person, my tired mind just not quite working fast enough.

'Oh, er, hello madam. Yes, patio doors and double glazing. I wondered if I could give you a free quotation. We have a special offer on this week for anyone who places an order before Friday . . .'

It was Barty. I leapt back but it was too late. He had seen me.

# Sixteen

A series of expressions followed each other across the alien's face.

'Oh, er, hello. I didn't know you were . . . That is, are you on the same job too, Dominic?' He hesitated and glanced at Granny Probity.

'You mean double glazing?' my grandmother enquired incredulously. 'He certainly . . .'

I interrupted her fast. 'Um no, Barty. That is . . . I certainly am.' I ushered him outside with an apologetic glance at Granny Probity. 'I'm giving them a quote already,' I whispered to Barty, and shut the door firmly and politely in my grandmother's face.

Outside, the alien turned to me, looking bewildered. 'I think there's some confusion here. We're supposed to be the ones who are checking up on those two Black Star Gang members, not you. Commander Parry definitely said we'd get double pay for doing unsociable hours, and she'd give the Bench Hellezine project more favourable consideration if we did just this one extra job whilst we were down here. I think you're the one who's made the mistake.'

'No no no, Barty.' I tried to calm him down, my mind racing. 'No, you've misunderstood. My colleague and I are here on a different mission. We're ...'

The door opened behind us.

'Dominic! Whatever are you up to? Come in at once and have your breakfast!' rang out my grandmother's voice. 'Are you still here, Mr O'Dawes? We don't want any double glazing and don't you try to talk my grandson into it.'

Slowly I closed my eyes, and when I opened them again both she and Barty were looking at me.

My grandmother just stood waiting for me to do as I was told. Barty put both his hands to his mouth and whispered, 'Oh ... oh ... no, I don't believe it ... !'

We were all incapacitated. Barty had fired his paralysing rays at myself, Granny Probity and Auntie in quick succession, then at Julia as she came down the stairs to see what all the noise was about. Now we were all slumped in armchairs in the living room, waiting for Scupper to arrive with Peter.

'Surely you don't need to brain-process them,' I said, trying to nod in the direction of the two elderly women. 'My great-aunt's memory isn't too good at the best of times. She won't give you away.'

'Oh yes I will!' snapped Auntie. 'There's nothing wrong with my memory and there will still be nothing wrong with it after you've done whatever you're going to do to me. You don't scare me, lad.' She glared at Barty. His fair skin reddened at her accusing and unwavering expression. 'Aren't you ashamed of yourself, young man?' she went on. 'Going round the universe attacking old women?'

Barty sighed and sat down. Auntie raised her eyebrows at him in a way that made him stand up again.

'You see, there are difficult moral questions here,' the alien explained in a plaintive voice. 'I am employed to do a job. On my planet we have developed a certain immunity to brain-processing, but that doesn't mean to say we should take advantage of it, and do less than our duty to the interplanetary community. If I hadn't accidentally revealed to Dominic certain secret information about the United Council of Planets' plan for Earth, there would have been no need for this. We would just have left you quietly to get on with your lives. Unfortunately I have no means of knowing how much he has told you.'

An instrument on his wrist began to beep.

'Sounds as if your cat's calling you,' I murmured.

The alien laughed, then controlled himself hurriedly.

'Yes?' He held the communicator to his ear. 'Good. We'll take them up two or three at a time.' He turned back to me. 'Scupper has got Peter. He was as shocked as I was to find out that you two were the Black Star members. I must say you terrorists are clever. It's a pity you're so extreme.'

'Barty . . .' I paused. Where were the words to tell this almost reasonable person that he was on the wrong side? 'Barty, can't you see that interfering with people's minds has to be wrong?' I asked him. It sounded weak and ineffectual.

Barty shook his head and polished his incapacitator on his sleeve.

'Where would people be, Dominic, if they were prey to all the wild, uncontrolled emotions that naturally inhabit their heads? I feel so bad myself, sometimes, that I wish I could be fully brain-processed and find peace.'

I struggled to move. I needed to go to the loo.

'Barty, where would people be – how can you ask me that? They'd be in the real world. Or worlds. They'd be properly human. Able to make properly thought out decisions. It's natural to feel bad sometimes. Everybody does. If you didn't feel bad sometimes how would you know when you were feeling good? They're only half alive, all those people out there in the rest of the galaxy . . .'

'Stop! That's enough!' He spoke sharply and sat down, despite Auntie's glare. 'I've heard about your Black Star propaganda, how effective it is. I won't listen to it.'

There was a sound outside. Scupper and Peter must be arriving. I felt despair. It would be only moments now before we were transported into space to have our brains picked clean and then obliterated.

I thought of Mr Batworthy, and of how the Council's computers would extract his whereabouts from my brain. After that there would be nothing to stop them from finishing Earth off completely. One more problem solved for the oh-so-efficient United Council of Planets. Another troublesome planet sorted. All in a day's work.

# Seventeen

'Oh good, Scupper's arrived,' Barty said. 'He can keep an eye on you all while I just search the house.'

My heart gave a jolt. The papers. Where had I put them? Oh no. When I had sat down to talk to Auntie I had simply dropped them on the floor next to my seat. They lay there now, half out of their folder, on top of Julia's copy of *The Beano*. Too late I averted my eyes. Barty had seen where I was looking. He bent, and swept them up in his hand.

'No . . .' I protested, knowing that such a remark was pointless. Barty began to study the papers with their coded alien messages. As he read them the colour drained away from his face. He looked extremely young with his hair falling over his forehead. He must only be a few years older than I was.

Granny Probity, who had appeared too shocked to speak since the incident on the doorstep, now groaned slightly. Julia and I both looked at her.

'Are you all right, Granny?' Julia asked in a tiny, frightened voice.

Granny Probity gave the slight nod which was the only movement any of us could manage. I felt rage that such indignity should be inflicted on these two old women. Barty spoke.

'Do you know what you've got here?' He waved the papers at me. I wondered whether it was strategically better to say yes or no. I wasn't sure what I had got, but my suspicion that it was the formula for a major time bomb seemed fairly likely to be right.

I decided not to answer, and just stared at him. Let him form his own conclusions. He went out of the room and I heard him opening the front door. There were voices. After a long delay Scupper came into the room. He looked round at us all, twiddling his gold earring. 'Peter's already in the gravity-blaster,' he remarked. 'They're sending down another so we can all go up at once.'

'I'm really disappointed in you two,' I said, remembering Mum's most effective method of mind control from years gone by. To have someone *disappointed* in one was the ultimate in depressingness. The number of times I had promised to do better after being told that one of my parents was disappointed in me went beyond counting. 'I really thought you were people who cared about others,' I went on. 'I really thought Hamshomis had the guts to stand up to the system.'

I was wasting my time.

'Shut up, Dominic.' Barty handed Scupper the papers.

'Are you *sure* that's what they are?' Scupper whispered, staring at them closely.

Barty nodded. His cat wove its way into the room and jumped on to my lap. Scupper stood very still, reading the computer printouts.

At last he said, 'Where did you get all this, Dominic?' I felt surprised that he did not know. Maybe they were not, after all, in on the Council's homicidal plans for our planet.

'Release us all with your incapacitator and I'll tell you,' I said. Granny groaned again and I looked at her with concern. Scupper glanced at his partner, then crossed the room to my grandmother and pointed his weapon at her. A green light glowed in the barrel and suddenly Granny Probity was moving about in her chair.

'Sit still,' Scupper said to her. Looking frightened, she did so. 'She'll be all right,' he added, glancing over at me. 'We can link her to a pulsar star with an electronic receptor while we take her up for brain-processing. It'll keep her heart going strong.' Then he swept his incapacitator round the room and released us all. I flexed my limbs and stretched, then stared at him, puzzled. Why did he feel confident enough to release us? It seemed ominous.

'Well then? Tell me. Where did you get these coded computer programs?' The black alien stood in the middle of the room with his hands on his hips.

Various plans of action flitted through my mind, but there was nothing that any of us could have done fast enough to avoid being put immediately out of action again. Anyway, what was there to lose? It wouldn't take them long to work out which computers I had access to. I just hoped that Mr Batworthy was safely out of sight in the basement.

'From our school computer,' I replied.

The two men looked at each other. 'Oh . . . I don't believe it,' said Barty for the second time that day.

Scupper shook his head as if in wonderment, and gave a short laugh. 'They're clever. You've got to hand it to them. They're clever, the powers that be. Who would ever have thought of looking here, on this backward planet, for the most advanced technology ever?'

'What is it?' I asked very quietly. Neither of them acknowledged my belated admission of ignorance, but Barty put his weapon down on the coffee table and sat on the arm of the sofa.

'Well, why shouldn't you know? We have to wipe your brains out now. No choice. Did you link up to these programs on your own?'

I nodded. 'Yes. No one else knows anything about it. I printed it all out to try and get some help with it.'

'Hm. Well, Dominic, these are the programs of Central Control. Somehow you have linked in to the central computer that controls all brain-processing everywhere. The whereabouts of Central Control is the most closely guarded secret of the civilised universe, and it looks as if the clever so-and-sos who rule our lives have located it somewhere here on this god-forsaken planet, where no one in their right mind would ever come, given the choice.'

Auntie gave an outraged gasp and Granny Probity, who seemed to be recovering, sat bolt upright in her chair.

I took a long deep breath as the information sank in. Central Control, the power behind brain-processing, here? No wonder the United Council of Planets could not blow us up. If they had blown up Central Control, no one would have been able to be brain-processed any more. Their entire mind control system would have crumbled, and with it their means of absolute unchallenged dominance over the planets. If they had blown up Central Control they would have become powerless. As indeed they would, if someone else were to do so.

# Eighteen

The aliens had left their gravity-blaster in a copse beside Home Meadow, rather than risk coming closer to the houses even with their invisibility screen on.

We must have made a bizarre sight, the four of us walking stiff-legged and rigid-armed up the lane. The aliens had paralysed just enough of us to prevent us from running away or shouting for help.

As it happened, the only person we did see was the postwoman in the distance, and she just gave us a cheery wave and climbed back into her van. Scupper and Barty walked one in front and one behind us, their incapacitators at the ready. Barty carried his unconscious cat under his arm. He had forgotten to remove it from my lap when he partially immobilised us again.

We turned the corner into the main road, and that was where it happened. It was one of those things that later you go over and over in your head, thinking how you could have handled it differently. How you *should* have handled it differently.

We had to pass the top of Home Meadow where Peter's goat still browsed among discarded Coke cans and thistles, beyond the fence. I automatically braced myself for its usual headlong charge. I was geared to do this because I had walked past it earlier. The aliens were not. Everyone else appeared too stunned with fright even to notice the animal.

With a reflex action, as the goat made its short dash, I stepped back. It looked like a goat in a cartoon, head lowered and legs pedalling. It hit the fence and everyone screamed and ran.

Immediately two gravity-blasters came skimming out of the trees. I rushed forward with a cry, as I saw what was going to happen, but it was too late. Julia, Auntie and Granny Probity were dragged into the spacecraft by the aliens.

In the panic, no one checked to make sure that we were all on board. The next moment the two gravity-blasters had revolved and vanished into the sky, hypo-relativity making nonsense of space and time, and I stood trembling and alone in the goat-blighted morning.

I walked. There seemed nothing else to do. I found myself moving zombie-like in the direction of the school.

The full enormity of what had happened tried to get into my head but I would not let it. I felt cold, hollow and unspeakably shocked. My family, kidnapped by aliens, was not a concept I could handle.

101

I went in at the side gate of the school and down to the basement in search of Mr Batworthy. He was asleep on Matron's mattress, among boxes of old books and some antique video equipment. He jumped up with a gasp as I approached him. I tried to find the words to say what had happened. Instead, when I opened my mouth, a great sob came out.

'What's the matter?' My teacher stood up fast. 'What's happened, Dominic?'

I told him. I also told him that the computer he had linked into was the United Council of Planets' central source of mind control.

'Oh . . .' He closed his eyes for a moment. When he opened them again his expression was intimidating. 'Then there is no time left. Now we must move, Dominic. Come!' He started to walk fast along the basement corridor to where the metal staircase led up to the gym. I hurried to catch him up. He shouted at me over his shoulder.

'Now we have to crack the code, Dominic. I have slept, and all is clear to me. We crack the code. We program the machine. We blow it up. In fact we make it blow itself up. It is only a machine. It will do as it is told. We are human and we shall defeat it.'

Despite the state I was in, prickles of excitement ran along my arms. Defeat it. Destroy the destroyer of minds. Fight it with itself. Suddenly it seemed possible. If only it could be done before my family's minds were destroyed.

We reached the computer room.

'You had better stay here with me, Dominic,' said Mr Batworthy as he seated himself at the console. 'They'll be searching for you now. They might have come straight back for you when they missed you. Anyway, you can do some of the calculations for me.'

I shook my head. 'I have to go, Mr Batworthy. I have to find a way of getting into space to try and rescue Julia and the others. I know where they'll have taken them. They'll be at the Alpha Centauri Interchange. I have to go back to the Old Rectory and see if there's some way there of getting into space.'

Mr Batworthy looked at me sadly. 'Stay hidden then, Dominic. Keep to the fields and hedges. Go safely.'

I left the school by the back door and cut through the woods. I moved from tree to tree, never knowing whether a gravity-blaster cloaked in its invisibility screen might be monitoring my progress and waiting to snatch me.

As I ran, stooped and furtive, I tugged gently at my left earlobe to activate my Black Star communicator, and called repeatedly in a soft voice, 'BS Eight to Black Star Gang. BS Eight to Black Star Gang. Come in any members of Black Star Gang. This is an emergency.'

At the edge of the woods I paused and looked over the field which I had to cross before I could once again be camouflaged by the copse, the haystack, the barn and then the garden wall. I poised myself to run fast. One quick dash seemed my best chance. The aliens might have come back at once when they recovered from their fright over the goat and realised their mistake in not taking all of us.

On the other hand they might have decided to brain-process those they had already and then come back for me afterwards. I took a deep breath and started to run. As I did so, two strong hands seized my shoulders.

# Nineteen

I half turned and simultaneously brought both my elbows sharply back before my brain had even properly registered fear or shock. The next moment I found myself looking down at a tall girl in jeans and a t-shirt, who was lying on the ground gasping with pain.

'Oh . . .' I was almost speechless. 'I'm . . . sorry. I thought . . .'

She tried to struggle to her feet. I put out my hand to help her. As I hauled her upright she touched her hand to her ribs and winced. She had short brown hair and green eyes.

'Look, I'm really sorry. But who . . . ?'

'Forget it.' Her voice was unfriendly. 'I'd heard you were a rough lot down here. I am here with orders from the leader. I just happened to catch your distress call as I flew in from Hare Moon, but you seem to be perfectly capable of taking care of yourself.'

I wanted to cry. Hare Moon, she had said. Now she was waiting for my reply.

'I'm sorry I hurt you. I get very jumpy because of . . . the silence.'

Her expression softened a little. Briefly I sensed warmth and even humour under her brusque exterior. The silence. Suddenly it seemed such a strange word. Have you ever heard or looked at a perfectly familiar word and suddenly it seems completely unfamiliar and strange? Try it now. Look at 'silence'. Odd, isn't it?

Why don't I just go to sleep now instead of writing all this? I think I must be overtired. I was overtired then, desperately overtired and in despair. There had seemed no one to help me in the entire world. Then I called into the silence and somebody came. I could hardly believe it.

The girl was looking at me with a frown. 'OK. What's your problem? You'd better make it fast. We're all being called in to help shift Bench Hellezine. I'm here to fetch you and BS Nine. The leader says you can fly a starship.'

'What?'

'Have you been brain-processed or something? You do know about Bench Hellezine, don't you?' She ran her hands through her short, shiny hair. Clearly patience was not her strong point.

'Look. Look . . .' I took her arm and led her back among the trees. 'Can we just get a few things straight? Yes, I know about Bench Hellezine. No, I can't fly a starship. Who is it thinks I can?'

'The leader.'

'Yes, you said it was the leader, but who precisely are we talking about? The new leader? Red Goff? We are a little out of touch down here, you know.'

'Shh.' She clapped a hand over my mouth and glanced over her shoulder. Her hand smelt of expensive soap. 'Yes. *How* out of touch are you? Do you know that the Council has refused to implement the Bench Hellezine plan?'

'No.'

'Ah. Well, they have, so now we're going to do it ourselves. We need all Black Star members, so can we please go quickly and collect BS Nine and be on our way?'

She drummed her fingers impatiently on a remote control strapped to her wrist, and briefly I saw the shimmer of a green gravity-blaster among the trees. She swore. 'I must stop doing that. Come on, BS Eight. What's the matter with you?'

So I told her.

She sank slowly back against a large oak tree as I came to the point where Peter and my family were abducted for brain-processing. She gasped as I told her that we had located Central Control.

'So can we please just get up to the Alpha Centauri Interchange? We may still be in time to save them. Bench Hellezine can wait.'

'Oh, Dominic . . .' The alien bit her lip and took hold of my hand. Her whole veneer of cold efficiency seemed to melt away. 'I'm so sorry. I would, but you see it would do no good. You obviously don't know, but the Starship Dupronic~has been docked on the dark side of your moon since yesterday. It has brain-processors on board. Your family will have been there and back long since. They will be at home already.'

'How terribly lovely to meet you, my dear,' said Auntie, shaking the alien's hand. 'What did you say your friend's name was, Dominic?'

'Pearce,' the tall girl replied with a sad smile.

Granny Probity put down the floorcloth she had been ironing and leaned forward. 'Would you care for a cup of tea, Pearce? Such awfully nice weather we're having.' When Pearce said yes, Granny Probity tittered with delight and swayed beamingly out into the kitchen, patting her hair as she went. 'Dear me, I must look an absolute fright . . .'

'Pearce. What a charming name. One of my favourites.' Julia dropped her *Beano* into the bin with an expression of distaste and sat in an armchair, straight-backed, with her knees and ankles neatly together. She tilted her head to one side and concentrated on our guest. '*Do* tell me all about yourself, Pearce.'

Auntie followed her sister into the kitchen, calling back merrily over her shoulder, 'Please excuse me. I mustn't let poor Probity carry that heavy tray all on her own. She's not strong, you know.'

She put out her hand in a gesture of refusal as I moved to help. 'No no, my dear. You three young things stay and chat together. It's delightful that you've brought a young lady home, Dominic. Why, you haven't brought a young lady home since Susan, or was it Louise?'

When they had gone Pearce raised her eyebrows.

'Well? Are they normally like that? I can see that I hardly need ask.'

I shook my head. I felt almost too shocked to speak. 'No.' I turned to Julia who was leafing through a wallpaper catalogue with fascination.

'My, but these patterns are so terribly pretty,' she was murmuring to herself over and over again.

'Julia, where's Peter?'

'Peter who?'

I bit my lip. 'Julia, you remember Peter. Peter Baxendale from Blackbarrow Farm?'

My sister wrinkled her brow. 'Vaguely. Give me more of a clue, Dominic. What does he look like?'

'He has red hair . . . oh, never mind, Julia. It's all right. Julia, can you remember where you have been for the past hour?'

She looked at me, puzzled. 'Of course, Dominic. I've been here. I've been helping Auntie and Granny Probity by doing a little dusting.' She smiled and arranged her skirts neatly over her knees. 'Have you had an interesting morning, Dominic?'

She seemed only mildly surprised when I crossed to her chair, hugged her and then burst into tears.

Pearce stroked my hair.

'Dominic,' she said softly. 'You say Batworthy is working on the destruction of Central Control. The best thing we can do in the meantime is to succeed at the Bench Hellezine project. If we move the planet it will be a great blow to the United Council. It will hit at their credibility and could be the start of their complete downfall. It could bring the Hamshomis over to us, if they see how strong we are. It could persuade the Myrions to accept our way of doing things, too, and to be of more use than they usually are.'

I thought of the Hamshomis, people like Barty and Scupper, already resistant to brainwashing, but conformers, unimaginative bureaucrats. I thought of the Myrions, rogue green giants, but blunderingly opposed to the United Council nonetheless. Did we really *want* these people on our side?

Yet ... perhaps this was what it was all about after all. Perhaps being civilised was all about being able to work co-operatively with a lot of other imperfect human beings with whom one did not entirely agree.

Pearce interrupted my thoughts. 'Anyway, you'll be safer almost anywhere else than here. They *are* going to be coming back looking for you, you know.'

I nodded and stood up. 'All right,' I said. 'Let's go and shift Bench Hellezine. But I warn you, I definitely don't know how to fly a starship.'

# Twenty

The sky was full of spacecraft. All around Bench Hellezine starships and gravity-blasters came like moths drawn from space towards the burning planet.

The airwaves were almost silent. 'Everyone is here,' whispered Pearce, 'but we don't want all this activity to alert the authorities.'

'What, you mean all the Black Star Gang are here?'

'What's left of us. They took a lot more people when they took BS One.'

We docked with a large starship.

'I don't know why the leader thought you could fly a starship. It's probably because Fenella Summerling seems to think you can do absolutely anything, so Red Goff must have assumed that included flying starships.'

'Oh.'

'Never mind. There's plenty more you can do.'

The ship seemed to be under the control of remarkably few people, all of them Black Star members, Pearce assured me, and all of them much older than me.

'Isn't Red Goff very young to be the leader?' I asked Pearce as we walked down a long corridor to the control and communications room. She shrugged.

'He's older than he looks. They age slowly and live a long time on his home planet. But yes, I suppose he is. Age isn't the main thing though, is it? He was the natural choice after his mother was seized. He has the same inventiveness. He's down there now on Bench Hellezine, talking on television and explaining what to expect during the planet move, and how it will stop the earthquakes and volcanoes and so on. It's important to reassure them. I think the move itself is going to be pretty frightening.'

I wondered about Fenella, whether she was down there too, whether she had still expected me to keep our appointment in the room over the tavern, and whether I would ever see her again.

In the large, circular control room I was introduced to Hals, a tall man in black. The room was full of people sitting at consoles, concentrating, speaking in low voices, adjusting controls. It was strange to be among only Black Star members, all of them previously unknown to me.

'Would you like to be the one to release the quark bomb, Dominic?' Hals asked me. 'It's fairly straightforward but it takes split-second timing. I'll be controlling the operation but I need another pair of hands. We need to get away fast, immediately after detonating the bomb. We're going to tow it into position on the sun side of Bench Hellezine now.'

I nodded, alarmed and awestruck. He explained that the blast of particles that would follow would combine with the pull of a magnetic net operated from the other side of the planet by its inventor, Benet Rogery, to shift the planet's orbit to safety.

Outside one window great flares roared off Bench Hellezine's sun. Outside another window the little planet itself, an elongated reddish brown rock, turned slowly. Its volcanoes were visible even from space. On screens all round the room its image was reproduced. It hung there, a tiny singed pebble, loaded with fragile humanity.

We towed the quark bomb into geostationary orbit.

'Now we must risk going on air to liaise with the other starship,' said Hals, sitting next to me at a bank of controls. He flicked a switch.

'Countdown,' said a voice I knew. 'Confirm countdown.'

'It is essential that you should count exactly together,' said Hals. 'Then press these two buttons simultaneously as you both reach nought.'

I put my hands on the controls and nodded.

'Countdown confirmed,' I replied to the distant voice, Fenella's voice.

'Dominic?'

'Hello. Counting now. Ten.'

'Nine.'

'Eight . . .' The numbers felt like a conversation. How are you? Are you taking care of yourself? Sorry I wasn't there.

I glanced out of the window. The quark bomb was just visible, in a line between Bench Hellezine and its sun.

'Seven, six, five . . .' Fenella and I counted together. Her voice sounded tense. Suddenly the screen beside me crackled and an unfamiliar voice filled the cabin.

'This is a United Council of Planets military starship,' yelled a woman's voice. 'Cease your countdown. This is Commander Parry. I order you in the name of the United Council to cease your countdown.'

I turned my head, still counting, 'Four, three, two . . .' and saw behind us, blotting out the galaxy, a massive silver monolith of a starship. It had orange stripes and black lettering along its side. STARSHIP HELISPEAR.

How had we not picked it up sooner? It must just have come straight out of hypervortex. Red warning lights flashed on and off all along the starship and two giant corrugated guns wagged from its front portals like reproachful fingers. If it had just come out of hypervortex its aim might not be so good. I took the chance.

'One.' I pushed the detonating buttons. 'Go,' I said to Hals in the same moment. A gigantic flash lit up space where Bench Hellezine had been and a buffeting particle wind shook our spacecraft like a dog shaking a bone. Then Bench Hellezine moved. We saw it move, then we ourselves were gone.

114

The rocketing rotation into hypervortex threw me across the cabin. I had forgotten to fasten my seatbelt.

When I sat up, stunned, space was streaming by like a wild, white flood.

'We did it,' said Pearce in a low voice as she stood up from her chair and helped me back to my feet. 'We did it . . .' Her voice was shaking. '. . . and if we can do that we can do anything. Earth comes next.'

The next fortnight was one of the strangest of my life. It was decided that, for my safety, I could not remain in Stoke Stiley. I must go into hiding for the time being. Consequently, for the next two weeks, I did not spend two consecutive nights on the same planet.

I went home briefly to tell Auntie and Granny Probity that I would be staying with friends for a while. I felt saddened and enraged afresh at their blank, accepting faces. Then I left Earth again fast and flew with Pearce in her gravity-blaster to a series of different worlds and a series of different safe houses of varying degrees of discomfort.

One night I slept in a cave on a planet that was icebound. I lay on the rock floor covered by a blanket made of thick animal furs, feeling, as my extremities froze, only the slightest twinge of guilt at the nature of my wrappings. Another night I slept in a Myrion's cellar, kept awake for hours on end by what sounded like a drunken orgy going on overhead.

Pearce did not always stay with me. By the end of the

first week I found that I had earache and a bad cold. I felt rather depressed and thought longingly of my own bed. I wondered continually whether Julia, Auntie and Granny Probity were all right, and worried desperately for the safety of Earth itself, centre of the galaxy's mind control. Presumably it would be safe so long as Central Control remained there. Once the mind controlling computers were removed, then perhaps nothing would be able to save us. If only we knew exactly where they were.

I met up with Hals again on one planet, and on another narrowly missed bumping into Commander Parry as she swept by with her bodyguards in a crowded street.

Towards the end of the fortnight I returned to Bench Hellezine and was introduced to the elderly scientist Benet Rogery, inventor of the planet shifting technique, who had joined the Black Star Gang just before we moved Bench Hellezine.

It was clear that the planet move had been a great success. Some areas had had rain for the first time in twenty years. Pearce and I walked once more along the dusty valley road towards the walled city of Stot, and I saw that a river now flowed under the city wall. Everyone we saw seemed extremely cheerful. A feeling of relief and exultation was in the air. I started to feel a little better. My nose stopped running.

We joined Benet Rogery on a sunny verandah on the outskirts of the city as the planet's sun, more distant now, went down behind a silent volcano. Pearce brought cool drinks similar to those I had first tasted in the tavern, and I thought of the old man who had believed that the end of the world was at hand. I thought of Fenella and Red Goff, but did not ask where they were. The slight lift that seeing the improvements in Bench Hellezine had given me, felt fragile and easily destructible. I thought I could probably let myself off hearing about the progress of Fenella's friendship with the new leader.

Benet Rogery told me that he had established contact with Mr Batworthy.

'Is he still hiding at the school?' I asked anxiously.

The old man shook his head.

'Oh no, he had to leave there. He's on the run like you are. Council guards came for him and he only just got out in time. But he had created the program he needed to.'

There was an edge of excitement in the scientist's voice. 'Now it's just a question of getting him back in there to program the machine to blow itself up. It seems as if the computer is not just linked to your school computer, but is actually physically close to it. We think it's almost certainly very deep under the school.'

I stared. My drink stood on the cane table losing its fizz. The computer that ruled the universe was under our school. I had been sitting on it for the past twelve years. People's brains were being destroyed during maths, French, chemistry, PE. As we worked, evil had been filtering up past our feet.

Benet Rogery was continuing. '. . . there is a natural cave structure in the Earth's substratum of rock there, and also some natural radiation which would, we think, supplement the reduced cosmic radiation at that depth. Council guards are surrounding the place at the moment, but they will probably be called off soon. The United Council thinks that Central Control is safe. They don't want to make anyone else think – least of all the Black Star Gang – that Earth is of any particular significance. That's the whole point of having Central Control in such an unlikely place.'

'So when the Council guards move out, is that when we move in?'

The old man nodded. 'We're moving more people down there all the time, but very secretly.'

That was when I knew it was time to go home.

# Twenty-one

Pearce was not a good driver. I was glad when our flight back from the centre of the galaxy was over and I stood once more in the meadow behind Peter's barn.

Earth looked beautiful. It was full of temporarily forgotten smells and sounds. The honeysuckle that clambered over the barn roof smelt like priceless scent. Long grass drooped in the heat, ready for mowing, misty with pollen. There was a heat shimmer on some old corrugated iron by the fence. In the distance I heard a thudding noise, possibly someone chopping wood, or maybe further impacts of the goat-without-brakes.

'At least the weather's dry,' said Pearce. 'You should be all right in the loft of the barn. Red Goff has Batworthy somewhere out in space at the moment, for safety, but he will be bringing him in later today.'

'Where will you be?' I followed her into the barn and we sat down on some old hay bales.

'I'll mostly be guiding people in. You'll probably be needed to get people into the school, since you know

119

your way round it. When Batworthy is back down here I think you'll be guarding him while he keys in the self-destruct formula. Don't go far away from the barn. It may be tonight.'

I shivered, despite the heat. Might we really, tonight, blow up the United Council of Planets' central computers?

'I'll be going up to the house to see my family, Pearce, and I want to see Peter Baxendale as well. I haven't seen him since he was brain-processed.'

'You'd be better not doing that, Dom.' Pearce took hold of my hand. Her green eyes looked very doubtful. 'They say . . . he's pretty bad. The computers did a much more thorough job on him than they did on your relatives. I suppose it was because of him being a Black Star member. Apparently his parents are so worried they've taken him to a psychiatrist. He scarcely knows who he is any more.'

I stared at her in horror. 'I didn't realise . . . I thought they would just have made him dopey and abnormally good natured like they did to Julia and . . .' There was a sound outside. I looked sharply towards the barn door. Pearce's nails dug into my hand as she too heard it. The sound came again, a faint rustle and a scrape, but further along. Someone was moving along the outside of the barn.

We were in shadow. The ripe smell of fermented grain surrounded us. The doorway was in bright light where the sun shone in at an angle. Motes of chaff floated in it. We listened.

Over in the copse of trees near the road, crows called. Their cries came and went as they circled then settled again. On the roof of the barn a pair of doves cooed unendingly. I tried to hear past these sounds.

Even though I was concentrating on listening, I felt a deep grinding sadness for Peter. So, despite everything, his brain had been destroyed. As mine would be, if the United Council were to catch me now. I must see him. I must see for myself if there was anything left of the friend I had known.

Pearce put her face close to my ear.

'I don't think it's anything.' She breathed the words almost soundlessly. 'But we'd better . . .' She nodded and eased her incapacitator out of its holster. Mine was already in my hand.

There was a creak from above and behind us. It came from the hayloft where high pale light filtered in through a small round window. Maybe it was just the winch creaking, over there in the shadows between the hayloft and the loading platform. I knew that winch. It was what I used to hold on to, to jump down from the hayloft, when I was small. The next moment it fled from my mind because there was a movement over by the door. I spun round. A shadow fell across the light. A figure shambled in. It was Peter.

'Peter!' I was stunned for a moment. Peter was bent, shuffling forward like an old man. I walked over to him.

He screwed up his eyes and peered at me, trying to adjust to the darkness. 'Peter! It's me, Dominic.'

He took a step back. 'Who?' He was clearly able to see me now, but his face contained no recognition. 'Who are you? What are you doing here? Don't you know that this barn is private property?'

I felt sick, and for a moment was too appalled to speak. Peter no longer wore his greatcoat. Instead he wore a white shirt and grey flannel trousers with neat creases down the front. At last I found my voice.

'Peter, surely you remember me? I'm your friend Dominic, BS Eight. This is Pearce. I'm so sorry I couldn't save you from the brain-processors, Peter. It all happened too quickly. I was too late.' I touched his arm. Pearce came and stood beside me. I saw that there were tears in her eyes. She put her arm around Peter. He shook it off.

'Get away. This barn is private property. You're trespassing on private land.' His brain seemed unable to encompass anything other than variations on this theme. His eyes were blank but accusing, the eyes of a bureaucrat. Pearce brushed her hand across her own eyes, then turned away, shaking her head at me.

'This barn is private . . .' Peter had begun mindlessly again, when there was a crash from the back of the barn. With a start we all turned to face the shadows, but before either Pearce or I could aim our incapacitators, the figure which had jumped down from the hayloft was facing us, its own weapon levelled. Its knees were bent, its arms extended. Both hands held the incapacitator.

'So now you see what we can do,' it said. 'You've seen your friend. Are you shocked?' The figure was unmistakeable. His gold earring caught the sunlight from the doorway. His black skin gleamed in the gold light. It was Scupper.

The three of us in the doorway had the disadvantage of being silhouetted against the brightness. I knew that neither Pearce nor I would be able to fire fast enough. It occurred to me that this might actually be the end.

Foolishly I tried the old trick of looking suddenly past him, hoping that he would think there was someone there, but knowing that Scupper was really far too intelligent to fall for that one.

I was astonished, therefore, when he slowly lowered his weapon, gradually relaxing his stance.

'Don't fire,' he said, as I raised my own incapacitator in amazement. He allowed his to drop from his fingers. 'See. I'm unarmed now. It isn't a trick. There's no one else here with me. I've given Barty the slip. I can't go on with this. Help me. I want to join the Black Star Gang.'

# Twenty-two

'I couldn't go on . . . it all started after we took your relatives up for brain-processing, Dominic . . . neither of us wanted to do it. I heard over my communicator what you said to Barty, when you were trying to stop us from taking them away, and I knew it was right. People's minds are their own. They shouldn't be brainwashed for the convenience of authority . . .' He stooped and picked up his incapacitator. Sharply I raised mine once more, holding out my other hand. After a moment's hesitation he handed me his weapon.

'Barty left you behind deliberately,' the alien continued. 'Did you realise that? It was quite easy to do in the confusion over the goat.' He glanced ruefully out across the fields.

'Oh really?' I stared at Scupper in disbelief. He began pacing round the barn.

'I saw Barty turning to grab you as we were hustling everybody on to the gravity-blasters. Then he just sort of shook his head and turned away and jumped on board and we took off. On the way up to the Dupronic I realised that that had been a turning point of some kind. We just, sort of, kept glancing at each other throughout the journey. It was unreal. We couldn't talk because of the other people there. I knew it was too late to save your relatives, but I realised then that I was going to try and join the Black Star Gang at the first opportunity. I thought Barty felt the same, but when we reached the Dupronic, Parry was waiting for us . . .'

Scupper shook his head and spread out his hands in a helpless gesture. 'She said she wanted to talk to Barty. He was gone a long time. I don't know what she said to him, but when he came back everything was different. He was . . . well it was as if he had been brain-processed himself, although I know that isn't possible.' There was the glimmer of tears in Scupper's eyes.

Pearce and I stood motionless as the Hamshomi stopped speaking. We paid no attention to Peter as he reiterated, 'This barn is private property,' and kept trying to usher us out. At last Pearce cleared her throat and spoke.

'We can't possibly trust him, Dominic.'

I stared at Scupper. I wanted to trust him. I believed him. He sighed, obviously interpreting my silence as doubt.

'Look, I know things,' he said. 'I never imagined this was going to be easy, but please give me a chance . . . I really want to help. Those papers from the computer – I've studied them now. I can hardly believe it myself, but . . . I know . . . exactly where the central computer is situated.'

I looked at him. My unwillingness to trust my own instinctive, positive reaction to Scupper made me sound cold. 'Really? Well, I'm afraid we all know exactly where the central computer is situated, Scupper. Is that the best you can do?'

Scupper looked disconcerted. He bit his fingernail. Finally he spoke again. 'I don't believe you. You mean . . . the Black Star Gang knows where Central Control is situated?'

I just raised my eyebrows at him.

'You know it's under the school?' he asked softly.

Out of the corner of my eye I saw Pearce jump up and briefly wave her fists in the air as if her team had scored a goal. We had been fairly sure, but this was confirmation, if indeed Scupper could be trusted.

Scupper looked baffled. 'Then . . . why haven't you done something about it?'

'I really can't say.' I kept my face expressionless. The alien's eyes narrowed.

'Oh . . .' he whispered. 'You're going to, aren't you? That's what this is all about . . .'

I did not reply. Scupper was a long way from being able to be trusted with secrets. Pearce pulled her left earlobe. 'BS Two?' she whispered. 'You'd better listen in to this.'

Scupper gestured towards me. 'Look, if that's what you're doing, then I want to help you more than ever. If

126

we could really just destroy Central Control . . .' His voice trailed off. Pearce and I looked at each other.

'What do you know about the United Council's plans for Earth, Scupper?' I asked him.

Pearce interrupted me. 'Dominic, this may be a trap. We mustn't forget that.'

I glanced back at Pearce. 'It may be a trap, but it may not. I always felt that Scupper didn't have his heart in it. We'll have to keep a very close watch on him if we rely on any of his information, but it could be too important to ignore.'

I sat down on a hay bale and Scupper did the same. 'Was there any more to your and Barty's mission than what you have told us?' I asked him. The alien leaned his head in his hands.

'There may have been . . . I suspected all along that Barty knew more than I did. On the surface we were supposed to be locating any gravity-blasters left behind from the previous Earth project, and keeping an eye on known Black Star members. You were all assumed to be too demoralised by the international situation here to do much, those of you who were left, and we were supposed to be making sure that you no longer had the means of getting into space. We were told that space would become ungovernable if you were all let loose.'

This tied in with what we already knew.

'Go on,' I said.

'Can you hear?' Pearce muttered softly to her communicator. She waited a moment then moved closer.

127

Scupper looked at her and for the first time smiled slightly.

'There were other teams down here besides us. They were mostly looking for Batworthy,' he went on, 'but that didn't concern us. Because Hamshomis aren't brain-processable we're not considered a hundred per cent reliable, so we're not given the difficult jobs . . . and, I've realised now, we're just given versions of the truth that would appeal to the worthy-minded.'

He stood up then sat down again, suddenly seeming very ill at ease.

'Their plans for Earth. OK Dominic, this is what I think their plans for Earth are, though I can't be sure. It took me ages to crack the code on those papers we took from you, and even now I'm not sure I've got it entirely right. But . . . I think they're going to relocate Central Control to some equally unlikely planet – you know those roadworks on the main Stoke Stiley road?'

We nodded. Traffic was regularly held up there and had been for the past fortnight.

'Well, that's what those are in aid of. They're digging underground to get to the main computers. Then, when Central Control is safely relocated . . .' He stopped and swallowed, '. . . they're going to destroy Earth completely. It will be a major meteorite strike, like the one that wiped out the dinosaurs, but worse. The plans for redirecting a large meteorite are finalised already, though they haven't started actually changing its course yet.'

There was a long, stunned silence in the barn. Outside, the crows were still clamouring. Across the field someone was calling the cows home. Scupper stood up once more and resumed his pacing round the barn, kicking at the dust and chaff beneath his feet.

'Why? What's the point?' I breathed.

Scupper shrugged.

'Well, they haven't been able to find Batworthy and they know he's going to publish the hypo-relativity formula to protect himself. That would enable Earth people to travel to the stars, and the Council are simply not willing to have you lot wandering around out there. From something Barty let slip, after his long meeting with Parry, I think it's called "Operation Spring Cleaning".'

Pearce and I stared at him.

'That's why I want to join the Black Star Gang,' Scupper added quietly.

# Twenty-three

Although I had not eaten all day, I did not feel hungry now. Scupper's horrific revelations had made food seem irrelevant. Nevertheless Peter, who slowly seemed to be trusting us more, went back to his house to bring basic food essentials like chocolate and crisps. I knew I should try and eat something. I might need all my strength later.

'Is it ever possible for brain-processing to wear off?' I asked Pearce, before she left to report directly to Red Goff. He had informed us that he was now waiting with Mr Batworthy on the dark side of the moon, and that the Black Star Gang from all over the galaxy was assembling in Earth's orbit, waiting for nightfall over Stoke Stiley.

Pearce shook her head in response to my question.

'I'm afraid not. I'm sorry, Dominic. It's not like getting back stuff that's gone into limbo on your computer, you know.' She sighed and patted my arm.

After she had gone, however, and Peter and Scupper

were sitting eating white chocolate flakes laced with caramel, Scupper raised the subject again.

'You know, Dominic, I think Pearce may be wrong about the brain-processing. When people on our planet, Hamshoma, were first becoming immune to brain-processing, they gave them huge doses that were supposed to be permanent, like they have done to Peter and your relatives. Some people were badly affected, temporarily, but they did all recover. I think it may be a part of Central Control's function to *maintain* people's brain-processed state. If so, then destroying the central computer might also destroy its effect on people.'

I felt a wild leap of hope in my throat. I looked out through the barn door to hide my sudden overwhelming emotion at the thought of Julia, Auntie and Granny Probity, abrasive and joking again, of Peter once more the person to whom I could say anything, no matter how ridiculous, and be understood. It was almost too much to hope for. It seemed impossible.

Across the field the first red darkening of the sky showed in the west as the sun tipped towards the horizon. Small bright clouds hung low and clustered together. Part of one vanished briefly and then reappeared. I gave a shiver as I understood what was happening. The gravity-blasters were coming in.

Swirls of wind were building up, eddying the grass, shifting the little bright clouds, threatening rain.

I was finding the need for maximum air silence oppressive. I knew that for safety's sake, in case any of us were captured, it was better that each of us should only know what we absolutely needed to. I could see the logic in that, but it did nothing to dispel my unease.

Moments later the summons came.

'BS Eight? This is BS Two. I am coming in with Batworthy in an hour. Black Star Gang members are gathering throughout the village. They will make their way towards the school and I want you to position them all around it. They will act as armed guards while Batworthy programs the computer. I also want you to take your relatives with you . . .' He paused.

'What?'

'I know it might look like taking them deliberately into danger, BS Eight, but we need to know immediately if the formula has worked.'

'What?' I repeated. 'You mean . . .'

'We need several brain-processed people so that we can observe them for signs of a return to normal brain function. Just one – your friend BS Nine – isn't enough. A few people do remain permanently damaged, though they are in the minority. So bring them with you, will you? They'll do as you tell them. Brain-processed people are very obedient. BS Eight? Are you there?'

I tried to steady my voice.

'Yes. Yes, I'll do that. So that means . . . BS Two . . . that your mother . . . ?'

'Yes,' he replied abruptly. 'OK. Do it. Contact me if there are any problems. Out.'

I realised that Peter was patting my arm. His expression was peevish. 'How many times do I have to tell you people?' he enquired. 'This barn is private property. You are trespassing, you know.'

I put my finger to my lips, unable to bear his repetitions any longer. 'Shh,' I said. 'I'll tell you what, Peter, you can come and trespass on *my* private property now. Fair enough?'

My friend shrugged in bewilderment. I realised sadly that I was already using the patronising tone of voice that one tends to employ to the mentally impaired. I glanced at Scupper and saw that his face was distorted by pity.

'OK,' I said to him. 'We're going up to my house. If you want to be of assistance to the Black Star Gang your first task is to look after Peter for the next few hours. Keep him safe and happy. Can you do that?'

Scupper nodded. 'It'll be a privilege.'

The little clouds turned into bigger clouds, blown by the rising wind, and it began to rain. With Peter and Scupper following me I skirted the edge of the fields, moving towards my house through the wet grass. We passed the bottom of the goat's field. The goat stared at us with its screwhead eyes but for once did not charge.

The field that backed on to our garden had been mown already and the barley stubble was sharp and blackened. Red Goff's cropped phrases bristled in my brain like the barley stubble under my feet. I looked back to where Peter plodded wordlessly behind me, and I dared not hope.

We reached my garden wall, all three of us wet now, water dripping from our hair and down our necks. Peter stood with his short red fringe plastered to his forehead, his expression one of complete bafflement as Scupper tried to keep him entertained with stories about Hamshomi cats and their cute habits.

We went into my garden through the wooden gate in the wall, walked along close by the fence and approached the back terrace obliquely. No lights were on in the house despite the greyness of the evening. The kitchen door and the french windows were all closed.

I peered into the dining room through the rain-spotted glass and saw to my shock that all of them, Julia, Auntie and Granny Probity, were sitting motion-less at the dining table. There was no food in front of them. They sat straight-backed with their hands in their laps. None of them moved. After I had been watching them for a few moments Auntie smiled and spoke to the other two. I could just catch her words if I strained my ears.

'It's turned out rather wet.'

The other two nodded vigorously.

'Yes, it's really quite damp,' Granny Probity agreed.

'Rainy, in fact,' added Julia. 'Such a change.'

Then they all fell silent again.

I stared in at them for several minutes. They looked so frail and insubstantial in the dim room, like drops of water themselves, held together only by surface tension.

Peter was stooping down beside me, wiping mud from his shoes with his handkerchief. I leaned down and looked into his eyes, trying to reach the remains of his poor mind.

'Peter, come on. We're going in. It doesn't matter about your shoes.' I tapped on the glass then opened the french windows.

# Twenty-four

As far as their mental states allowed, all three of them seemed pleased to see us. They did not appear to have noticed my absence particularly, and they donned their macintoshes and followed me out into the rain without question.

'I don't seem to have been this way for a while,' remarked Auntie as we turned out of the lane and into the main road. 'Where are we going, Dominic?'

'To the school,' I replied, glancing around continually for signs of any Council agents.

'Oh, is it parents' evening? Have you been a good boy, Dominic?'

I saw Scupper grin.

'No Auntie,' I answered, 'it's something different. You'll see.'

I hoped she would. Oh, how I hoped she would see.

We reached the school and I left all five of them in the dryness of the school's front porch. After a moment's hesitation I returned Scupper's incapacitator to him.

'I hope you won't need it. You'd better have been telling the truth, Scupper. I'm trusting these people to you. They can't look after themselves.'

Then I left them and walked the length and breadth of the village as the Black Star Gang appeared out of the twilight. They came marching silently along the main road through the village, squelching through the mud along the towpath, appearing from their invisible gravity-blasters in the woods like chained spirits from trees. There were faces I knew from the Bench Hellezine mission, Hals and others, and faces I did not know at all, men, women and people my own age.

Residents of Stoke Stiley, drawing their curtains as darkness fell, looked out of their windows in surprise. A farm labourer going home on his bike stopped and watched.

'We don't often get demonstrations in Stoke Stiley,' he remarked, noticing me standing nearby. 'What's this in aid of then?'

'Oh . . .' I smiled at him. 'It's an ecological thing, you know, to save the Earth.'

He shook his head and clicked his tongue. 'Arty farty nonsense that is and no mistake. They'd be better off digging the earth rather than saving it, if you ask me. Soon get it out of their systems, that would. Be too tired to demonstrate if they did a bit of honest labour for a change.' He climbed back on his bike and went on his way.

The hour was nearly up. I guided the Black Star members into position round the school, showed them the ways through side gates and gaps in hedges and fences, until the building was surrounded by a ring of silent figures, weapons in their hands. Then we waited in the rain for Red Goff and Mr Batworthy.

The black gravity-blaster appeared where the last streak of purple light showed below the heavy clouds in the west. No one made a sound, but it felt as though a silent collective sigh rose from around the school. This was it then.

Mr Batworthy looked exhausted, but not as bad as he had the last time I saw him. He greeted me with a firm handshake and a very warm smile. I was pleased to see Pearce emerge from the gravity-blaster behind him. We went into the school.

'First of all I want to call up the neural imaging of the underground computer,' Mr Batworthy said as he seated himself at the terminal. 'I must be sure that no one is there who could be harmed by the explosions. I doubt very much that there would be. I think this is a machine that works very much on its own.' He started to tap at the keyboard.

Peter and my relatives were now seated at school desks at the back of the room, closely watched by

Scupper. Red Goff and I stood looking over Mr Batworthy's shoulder.

'Where's BS Fourteen? Is she all right?' I asked under my breath. Red Goff looked faintly amused at the irrelevance and untimeliness of my question.

'She's fine. She's armed to the teeth and guarding the roadworks with a few others, in case the Council realises what we're up to and tries to take Central Control out fast. I don't think they could, but you never know.'

I was appalled. 'But isn't that terribly dangerous?'

'Can you think of any part of this which isn't terribly dangerous?'

A picture appeared on the screen. It showed a small room with banks of controls along the walls. Thousands of tiny lights winked on and off. Mr Batworthy tapped the keyboard and the imaging moved in closer. Each tiny light had a numerical code above it. Mr Batworthy looked at his notes.

'Those correspond to the codes for each of the brain-processing centres on the planets and space stations,' he said after a moment. He moved the imaging in closer still, and suddenly we were inside the machine itself, where coloured beams leapt and flashed.

'Artificial neurotransmitters,' he muttered. 'You are now seeing the equivalent of what goes on inside your own brains all the time.'

The silence in the room was absolute. Outside the rain drummed on the roof and the rising gale smashed against the windows. On the screen we came out of the machine and Mr Batworthy panned once more round the small room which contained it, shown in angular, spectral detail on the computer screen. There was no one there.

'Very well then.' My teacher looked around at us, as he had done during many a lesson in the past. He smiled over at Auntie.

'Isn't that Mr Batworthy?' Auntie asked Julia.

'Oh yes,' replied Julia primly. 'Such a terribly nice man.' Pearce sat down with them and smiled at Scupper.

The moment extended.

'Very well then,' repeated Mr Batworthy, and peered at his notes.

He spoke rapidly and keyed at the same time, as he often did when teaching. It was a skill I had long admired and tried to copy, without success. 'What I am doing is persuading the machine to disable itself. In effect, it will be brain-processing itself in the same way it has, for example, brain-processed Peter. There will be small explosions, but I'm not sure they will be able to be felt here. There will be three, and if we are going to hear them, we should be hearing the first one about now.'

No one moved. It seemed as if no one even breathed.

Suddenly the ground shook beneath our feet. Granny Probity screamed and Scupper gasped. Then the ground shook again. There were shouts from somewhere outside.

I saw to my astonishment that there were tears on Mr Batworthy's face.

We waited. Three, he had said.

'Come on, come on,' he whispered and drummed his fingers on the table. Nothing happened. He picked up his notes and scanned them frantically. Then the ground shook again.

# Twenty-five

I crossed to the back of the room. We all did. The four brain-processed people did not look at all surprised or disconcerted as we stood and stared hard at them. They all just stared back.

'Is it time to go home now, Dominic?' asked Granny Probity.

'It's been a delightful evening. Thank you so much,' piped Julia.

Auntie smiled beatifically. 'Delightful. A delightful evening. I do enjoy these parents' evenings.'

I thought I was going to be sick. Pearce put her hand on my arm.

'I told you it wasn't going to make any difference to them, Dominic,' she whispered. 'You should never have hoped. Never mind. It will have helped others. Just think of all those it will have saved in the future.'

'This school is private property,' said Peter. 'Are you sure we should be here?'

I turned to Mr Batworthy. 'Has it worked?' I asked

him harshly. 'Can you tell if Central Control has actually been destroyed?'

He was already calling up the neural imaging again. The tiny underground room appeared once more on the screen. It looked the same until one noticed the slight blackening around the control panels, and a warping and distortion at the centre. Mr Batworthy moved the imaging inside the machine again. Here, shockingly, there was only a blackened, twisted mess. No coloured beams flashed now. No artificial neurotransmitters mimicked the brain's messages.

'It worked,' he said flatly. He looked over at the sad row at the back of the classroom. 'I'm so sorry it didn't help them, Dominic.' I could tell there was an elation in him that he was trying hard to suppress out of sympathy for me. 'But just think, as Pearce says, they can't do this to anyone else now.'

But Red Goff was shaking his head. He looked sharply round the room.

'There's something wrong,' he said. 'It hasn't worked for *any* of them. By the law of averages that's abnormal. You're wrong, Pearce. This sort of extreme brain-processing relies on continual supplementation. Destroy the machine and you destroy the brain-processing . . .'

At that moment there was another explosion, but this time it was close to us. We all jumped and seized our weapons. There were running footsteps in the corridor outside. I was raising my incapacitator to fire, as the first orange-uniformed guards burst into the room.

There were too many of them. They rushed in, dozens at once. A few fell, stunned by our incapacitator beams, but then we were overrun. My arms were pinioned behind my back.

'Sorry,' said Pearce, and pointed her incapacitator at my head. I stared at her in disbelief, then slumped back. She gave a rueful shrug. 'It was fun while it lasted,' she added.

Within moments all of us in the room had been taken captive.

In the silence that followed, the sound of tapping footsteps came along the school corridor. They reached the open door of the computer room and I watched as a figure with very wide-spaced eyes and bright red hair, my old enemy Commander Parry, came into the room. She was followed by two guards dragging Fenella between them. They draped Fenella over one of the desks. I saw that she was unconscious. Behind them came Barty, carrying the beeping cat under his arm.

Parry was smiling. She began to laugh.

'Oh, how amusing.' She shook her head. 'All this drama.' She came further into the room and sat on the edge of one of the desks. 'Did you really imagine that we would let the Black Star Gang destroy Central Control? Still, it kept you all quiet for a while, didn't it? Oh dear me, and it was such *fun* rigging up those *artificial* artificial neurotransmitters.' She appeared to be convulsed with laughter. 'Oh my, I haven't had such a good time in years.' She slapped her red-trousered thigh and guffawed. Then she turned to Barty and her tone hardened.

'Are all those outside being removed?'

I heard Red Goff give a faint groan. Barty nodded.

'Yes, commander. We're doing it now. They're all being ferried up to the Alpha Centauri Interchange for brain-processing. It was a brilliant idea of yours to get nearly all the Black Star Gang together like this.'

I caught sight of Scupper's grief-stricken face, and realised what the loss of his friend must mean to him. I knew, too, that I had been right to feel I could trust him.

Commander Parry was beaming modestly at the flattery.

'Thank you, Barty. It was nothing really. Once Pearce had told us of the Black Star Gang's plans to destroy Central Control, all we had to do was move it to safety, then wait for them all to arrive.'

The alien commander clapped her hands together and raised her voice. 'All right, most of you guards can go and help with the transportation. Just leave three guards per prisoner. I find it's always wise to be numerically on the safe side with the Black Star Gang. We'll wait a little while until the first rush of transportations is over. You can release that Fenella girl now. She looks awfully untidy sprawled about like that, and I'd really like her to hear what I have to say.'

One of the guards aimed a green incapacitator beam at Fenella's head. She moaned and stirred.

'Let me help her,' I begged. My two captors just laughed and held my arms even more tightly, but the guard who had released her helped her into a chair. Fenella looked round the room then sank her head into her hands.

'Are you all right?' I called out to her. She looked up at me and tried to smile.

'I gather they put up quite a fight at the roadworks,' commented Parry drily.

Auntie, Granny Probity, Julia and Peter were still sitting patiently at the back, looking only mildly surprised at the presence of a roomful of armed aliens. Mr Batworthy, closely guarded, sat with his back to the computer terminal, staring white faced at the far wall. Parry turned to me.

'Did you honestly think that we'd leave our central computer where you people could find it, Dominic? Oh yes, it was here for a while, hidden under the school. We were quite surprised when you managed to track it down. But did you imagine it wasn't transportable? Did you imagine we wouldn't have the means of moving it quickly to a place of safety? And did you seriously imagine, once it was out of its shell that you have so wantonly destroyed, that it would actually *look* like a computer?'

Her all-encompassing gaze swept round Red Goff, Fenella and me. She sighed.

'You're clever young people. I'm going to offer you a way out of this. We need clever young people whose brains haven't become too dulled. I'd like to offer you a job.'

She paused to allow this to sink in. 'Jobs are going to be in short supply on Earth soon, even shorter supply than oxygen, food and water. This would be an opportunity for you to be of service to the civilised universe, Dominic. All of you. You've shown what you can do.'

She stood up and walked round the room with a measured tread.

'We need spies, basically. We're realistic. We know we will always have dissenting groups, though we hope that none will ever become such a pain in the neck as the Black Star Gang were. Your job would be to infiltrate such groups and report back to the United Council.'

She stopped in front of me. 'You would have to agree to leave Earth for ever, Dominic, but then, Earth is not going to be a very pleasant place to be, soon.'

She turned to include the other two once more. 'You would all have to agree to a little sensible, low level brain-processing. Sorry Scupper, this rules you out. To be reliable, you would have to agree, genuinely, to what we are asking you to do, then your agreement would be planted permanently in your brain, as part of the brain-processing. You would not be able to go back on it or deceive us. However, you would retain a privilege that only very few are allowed. You would be permitted to remain quite alert and inventive and you could keep your sense of humour. You'd be rather as I am. Wouldn't you like that? This was what we did with Pearce.'

There was a stunned silence. 'It's the best possible deal you can get out of this situation,' Parry added. 'Perhaps you'd like a few minutes to think about it.'

Fenella stood up, ignored the guard who tried to grab her, and came and stood by my side. This time she managed a real smile. She turned it on Parry.

'Yes, we can certainly see that you have retained your sense of humour, Parry,' she said.

Parry looked angrily from Fenella to Red Goff and me. 'Does she speak for all of you? Are you really refusing this chance?'

Red Goff stared at her scornfully. 'I would rather be dead than be like you, Parry.'

I gave a mock-regretful sigh. 'Sorry Parry. What you're offering makes Earth after a meteorite strike sound positively enticing.'

The three of us and Scupper looked around at each other, and for a moment I felt brave and strong again.

# Twenty-six

'Come on then,' said Parry in a tired voice.

'For goodness' sake let's get them out of here. We have the Black Star Gang and Batworthy too. It's been a good day's work . . .'

Mr Batworthy interrupted her. His voice sounded creaking and ancient. He looked ill.

'Commander Parry, I accept that you have won, and that I am now in your power, but as a scientist, might I just ask you one or two questions about the real computer? Purely as a matter of academic interest?'

'Oh, I don't see why not,' said the alien commander. 'I do admire your talents, Batworthy. What would you like to know? It can't possibly do you any good since we will be wiping your brain completely clean once we have extracted what we want from it.'

Mr Batworthy frowned. 'Just how advanced is your central computer, Commander Parry? It must be something quite remarkable. What level of development has it reached?'

Parry smiled, a little, secret smile. 'It can think,' she said quietly.

I leaned forward, straining against my captors' grip. 'Think?' I asked.

'Yes, think, Dominic. Not a process you're terribly familiar with after all, it seems.'

'You mean, think independently, like a person?' Mr Batworthy's voice was incredulous.

Parry gave a small, smug nod. 'At one point we became a little concerned,' she confided. 'We thought it was starting to be able to feel, too, but that was just a false alarm.'

'Feel?' Mr Batworthy croaked. 'You mean, feel emotions?'

'Precisely, but as I say, it was just thinking more independently. Emotions would be another matter. Emotions make for instability.' She sighed deeply and extended one hand, palm upwards. 'It's tiny, Batworthy. Smaller than a human brain. Tiny enough to hold in my hand, if it had been tangible. However it is nothing so gross or unsubtle as a material thing. It is a force field. We move it with magnetic tongs. It needed an extensive support environment at one time, but now we have found a better way of . . . wiring it up. A way that reaps additional advantages and gives it a whole range of new opportunities for initiative . . .'

My mind reeled with shock. I felt cold and suddenly completely helpless. An invisible computer with initiative? A force field that could think for itself and govern the way others thought? A formless device with ideas? This went beyond terror. The powers of such a force might be limitless. And we, the Black Star Gang, were back at the beginning, no nearer than we had ever been to eliminating the monstrous Thing that enslaved people's minds all over the universe.

Parry was still talking. '. . . there may be minor disadvantages in its present location, as far as its vulnerability is concerned. We shall see, and learn as we go. That's one reason we needed to deal with the entire Black Star Gang quickly, so that you couldn't remain a danger to it. However, the advantages of its present siting override all possible disadvantages. The new powers it has acquired are proving truly awesome.'

She rubbed her hands together. 'Anyway, that's enough of that. It's time to take you miserable lot up to Alpha Centauri and stop you from either thinking or feeling.' She gestured to the guards to remove us.

As they moved towards us, something crossed my mind. Parry had a possessiveness, a personal pride in this central computer, that was clearly immense. Was it possible, I wondered, that she might be keeping it near her, in its new incarnation, to monitor its performance and the progress of its frightening new powers?

Then the thought went from my mind as the guards seized hold of me. They paused as Parry's voice rang out once more.

'Oh, there is just one more thing you might like to

know about our central computer.' There was a pitying smile on her face. 'It is, actually, indestructible . . .'

She was chuckling as the guards dragged us out of the room. There was mud on the floor of the corridor. We all skidded and slipped in it as we tried to stop ourselves from being hauled out to the waiting gravity-blasters. Julia, Auntie, Granny Probity and Peter just trailed along behind.

'Dominic, do get up. You'll get your trousers muddy,' called out Auntie.

'Auntie!' I yelled. 'Ring the police! Dial nine nine nine, Auntie! I'm being kidnapped!'

Auntie frowned, bewilderment on her face.

'What does he mean?' she asked Julia. I moaned and held desperately on to the front doorhandle. The door swung and hit one of the guards in the face.

'I'm going to stun him,' snapped the guard angrily. 'We'll have to carry him.' But then there was a sound. We all heard it. Everyone stopped and guards and prisoners listened together. It was a siren.

The sound came and went in between the great gouts of wind and rain that crashed into the school porch.

Parry swore. 'Get them into the gravity-blasters fast. I don't want to have to brain-process half the Somerset police force as well. We've got far too many to do already.'

'Hold on!' I shouted to Fenella. She was already holding on. Both her hands were locked round the other

152

doorhandle. One of her guards raised his weapon but suddenly Barty was in front of us.

'Stay there,' he said. His cat was peering out from the neck of his jacket. 'I'll go and talk to them. Let's just try and put them off. There's a crowd of villagers outside. We've had quite enough violence for one day.' I looked beyond him and saw that several people were visible beyond the school fence. One of them looked like the farm labourer to whom I had spoken earlier. He was pointing triumphantly in the direction of the siren.

To my surprise Parry inclined her head at Barty's suggestion. 'Go on then. You might have to do more than just talk to them, though.'

'Yes, I know.' He sighed. 'But just an illusion or a very mild scrambling of their brainwaves might do the trick.'

Parry frowned but nodded. 'Oh, well, all right.'

He walked out into the road.

The rain was like a solid sheet of water and the headlights were dazzling. The accident happened before anyone even recognised the danger.

# Twenty-seven

One moment we were all peering through the wind and rain in the direction of the siren, the next moment Barty was lying in the road, mown down by the skidding police car. He hadn't stood a chance.

People were screaming. Then the lights went out, all the lights, everywhere, at once. As far as the eye could see was utter blackness. I had the ridiculous feeling that all the lights in the world had gone out in that moment.

'Help!'

'What's happened?'

'Where are you?'

I could hear the sounds of panic in the street outside. The street lights, the school lights, the lights in the houses, had all failed at once. It must be a major power cut.

'Oh no! Oh no!' Parry was shouting as she rushed past me in the darkness. Both my guards let go of me in the confusion. I stumbled out into the night. I did wonder for a moment if I had gone blind, but no, everyone was crying out that they could not see.

'What on earth's going on?' yelled a voice behind me. It was Auntie's. 'What the dickens am I doing out here in the pouring rain in the middle of the night with all the lights off? Have I sleepwalked again or something?'

'What's happened? Help! Who's there? How did I get here?' It was Julia, panic-stricken. My heart thudded wildly. I blundered about, trying to find them in the darkness, shouting out their names. I couldn't believe that they sounded like their old selves again. It seemed like a trick of the darkness.

'Auntie! Julia!'

A torch beam flickered, beyond the school fence. Two policemen were stumbling towards where Barty lay in the road.

'Oh no . . .' said one in horrified tones. 'I think we've killed him.' Another torch was produced. 'There's no pulse.' He called quickly on his radio for an ambulance. As I pushed my way forward I saw in the wavering torchlight that Parry was trying to get to Barty.

'Leave him! Leave him alone, you there!' she shouted. 'He'll be all right!' The two policemen ignored her.

'Stand back, you silly old fool,' said the farm labourer. 'You're only hindering them. There's no way that one is going to be all right again.'

Parry turned on him a truly frightening glare. 'You don't understand, imbecile,' she hissed. 'He will recover without their help. A little accident like that can't harm him.'

The two policemen were crouching down by Barty. The crowd dragged Parry back and the guards, dimly glimpsed in the darkness, seemed to be milling about in disarray.

'You give him mouth-to-mouth,' I heard the first policeman say as I edged closer. 'I'll try and get his heart started. It's a nasty head injury. Go carefully.' They worked on Barty's motionless form. Someone brought blankets from a nearby house. In the shadows surrounding the torchbeams, everyone watched.

'I've got a heart beat.' The policeman's voice was jubilant, and as he spoke the street lights came back on.

'He's started breathing on his own. Thank God.' There was overwhelming relief in the second policeman's voice.

Suddenly the guards seemed to remember what they were supposed to be doing, and they started trying to grab their prisoners again. However, they were strangely easy to push away. I saw Fenella give one of them a mighty shove, and he fell into the mud and just lay there. It was as if they were on half power.

The whole scene was rapidly turning into a riot. One of the policemen barged in, trying to restrain people.

'Now then! Now then! Come along there! Calm down!'

I heard the other policeman calling on his radio for reinforcements. I eased my way out of the crowd and moved closer to Barty. Auntie found me and took my arm, looking a little anxious.

'It was so kind of you to invite me,' she said, 'but now I'm rather wet and I think I'd like to go home, if it's no trouble.' I stared at her in dismay.

'Auntie, you were all right . . . just now . . . when the lights were off . . .'

In the roadway, Barty suddenly sat up. The guards appeared to be regaining their strength. Prisoners were seized and whole swathes of people fell, immobilised by incapacitator beams, as the aliens abandoned subtlety. I looked from Auntie to the street lights to the guards to Barty. Fenella and Scupper appeared at my side, panting.

In the roadway, Barty eased himself up on to his knees and winced.

'Well I'll be blowed!' exclaimed the farm labourer. 'He's recovering. It's a miracle.'

Parry thrust me to one side and stood over Barty with her hands on her hips. 'Just wait until I get my hands on the idiot who bungled his armour plating,' she hissed. She looked at the farm labourer who was still exclaiming his astonishment. 'Of course he's recovering, you stupid little man,' she shouted with a mad cackle. 'Of course he's recovering! He's indestr . . .' Her eyes met mine. Her voice dropped abruptly and trailed away. 'He's . . . indestructible.'

# Twenty-eight

The wind and rain were slackening off. Visibility became better. My drenched clothes hung on me. Parry's gaze remained fixed on mine. There was the sound of more sirens. I took a long, shaky breath.

'Oh . . . surely not,' I said when at last I could speak. I felt Fenella's and Scupper's shocked stillness next to me. In the roadway, to gasps from some of the crowd and remonstrations from one of the policemen, Barty rose to his feet. Parry raised her eyebrows at me and turned away.

'Come on, Barty,' she murmured. 'You may have a self-repair facility in your new brain, but you're going to need a bit of an overhaul after this. Come on, quickly into one of the gravity-blasters. I want you safely out of this disturbance.'

He walked obediently towards the gravity-blasters in the playground, away from the crowd, and Parry turned her attention to the riot. 'Guards! You'd better bring everyone up. The entire village, I think. Dear me, I could do without this extra workload.'

But all around us the riot was gaining momentum and people were not that easy to catch. For a moment both policemen watched their patient, who was now clearly no longer in need of their attention, then they began trying to restore order. Incapacitator beams flashed and both policemen fell. Parry had moved away and was speaking into the communicator on her wrist, presumably also calling for reinforcements.

While her attention was diverted I ran to stand in front of Barty.

'Is it true?' I asked him. My brain struggled with the enormity of the question and its possible answer.

He looked back at me with his bright blue eyes and nodded once.

Fenella joined me, standing in front of him, and looked closely into his eyes. 'You mean ... Central Control is ... in your head?'

He nodded again.

Wordlessly Scupper bent down and picked up Positron, the beeping cat, who must have been thrown clear during the accident and was now cowering nearby. He stood up with the animal in his arms, and looked his friend in the face.

'I can't believe it,' he whispered.

Barty shook his head and glanced away.

'It was when we took Dominic's relatives up, wasn't

it,' Scupper said. 'That was when they put this computer into your head, wasn't it. I knew something had happened, but . . . not this.'

Barty nodded again.

'Couldn't you have found a way to stop them somehow?' Scupper persisted in anguished tones.

'*Stop* them?' Barty whispered. His voice was filled with scathing incredulity. He tried to push past Scupper. I checked to make sure that Parry's attention was still elsewhere, then took hold of Barty's arm. I am holding Central Control, I said to myself, and was swamped with disbelief.

Two guards approached us then.

'Come on, sir!' they shouted. 'We have orders . . .'

Fenella picked up a dropped incapacitator and floored them with its flickering red beam. But even while they were in the process of falling, four more guards rushed at us from behind. Beams flashed and flared and the men slumped in a heap. Turning, I saw Red Goff and Mr Batworthy running along by the fence, weapons raised.

Barty looked around him, then started to walk away from the direction of the gravity-blasters. Scupper rushed to his side and walked with him. The rest of us followed. I glanced back but could not see Parry any more. Presumably she must think that Barty was being safely escorted into space.

'Barty, I can't believe this. I can't believe you're now responsible for all that brain-processing,' cried Scupper. 'Have you no control over it? Can't you just not do it?'

Nearby, ambulances were arriving and paramedics jumping out of them. None of the rioting crowd took any notice of them. Barty spread his hands helplessly.

'It's like another person in my head,' he said at last. 'It does what it is programmed to do, but sometimes I have the strange impression that we overlap, that it is me and I am it.'

The commotion was growing wilder behind us.

'Where are we going?' asked Scupper.

Barty went on speaking. 'I seem to blend with it, add something to it . . .'

'Initiative,' I murmured. 'Initiative and flexibility are what you add. You're the new support environment that gives it extra powers.'

Barty stood still suddenly. 'But why me?'

Mr Batworthy, puffing slightly, caught up with us and shook his head.

'They needed a strong brain, Barty, not one addled by repeated brain-processing. You were the ideal receptacle for this unimaginably powerful force field. It had to be a Hamshomi, the only non-brain-processed people who are obliging, law-abiding and unrebellious.'

Barty looked round us all. He breathed in deeply and his eyes narrowed.

'Yes,' he said slowly. 'I am powerful. I can feel that I am powerful.' Subtly his voice changed. It almost seemed to have an echo in it. 'Oh yes, I am very powerful . . . more powerful than any of you can imagine. More powerful than Barty can imagine. Moreover, with Barty's help, I now appear to be able to do that which I am not programmed to do.'

A gasp ran round the small group of us.

'Oh . . .' whispered Fenella. She spoke for us all, as we realised that what we were hearing was the voice of Central Control.

'What . . . what can you do that you are not programmed to do?' asked Red Goff softly.

'Well, Parry isn't following us for a start, is she?' replied the Voice.

Mr Batworthy stepped forward. He seemed to be shaking with excitement. 'Tell me, can you really think? Can you feel?' he demanded.

The Voice that issued from Barty's lips was faintly amused. 'Yes, Batworthy, I can certainly think, and I can probably feel, if I have understood correctly what that means. I feel friendship for Scupper and fondness for Barty's cat. I dislike Commander Parry immensely. I feel . . . regret . . . at the state of your relatives, Dominic. Unfortunately, this capacity to feel is probably only a malfunction, and there will always be someone who will mend me. I am, after all, only a machine, and ultimately I shall have to do what I am programmed to do. And I shall have to do it for ever, whether I want to or not, because I am indestructible.'

I saw that Barty's lips were trembling and his eyes were wide and terrified now. I felt an overwhelming longing to rescue him from this Thing inside him, but I knew there was nothing I could do.

The Voice continued. 'I deliberately caused the technician to build a weakness into Barty's armour plating.' His voice was lower now. It was quieter here. 'I am . . . so tired . . . of all this.'

Suddenly there were pounding feet. Parry and several of the guards had burst from the crowd and were rushing towards us. We had reached the corner of the school's perimeter fence where another police car now stood, empty, its occupants also presumably trying to deal with the riot.

Barty stopped by the police car and looked back. A look of intense concentration came over his face and Parry and the guards slowed in their tracks.

'So . . .' I said carefully, 'you are saying that you, the computer, have acquired a new function. You have learned how to make independent decisions. So, you could choose to do anything?'

Barty stroked his cat where it nestled in Scupper's arms, and for a moment he looked comforted. When he spoke again the voice was so faint that I could not tell whether it was his or the computer's.

'It might be interesting to find out, Dominic,' he replied. For a moment we stared into each other's eyes. 'If all brain-processing facilities were out . . . even for a little while . . . who knows what might happen?' He whispered it. I heard it in my head, but I did not see his lips move. Briefly he touched his forehead as if it hurt. Then he bent and stepped abruptly into the police car.

# Twenty-nine

As Barty pulled the car door shut after him, Scupper rushed forward to join him. 'Barty, if you're going into hiding, I'm coming with you.'

He dragged at the passenger door but the car started to move before he could get in. It accelerated jerkily in a wide arc, bumping up the pavement and down again. There were gasps from the crowd. Parry, released from her unnatural stillness, rushed forward as she saw what was happening. The passenger door, wrenched open by Scupper, flapped wildly as the car gained speed. Some guards and a few other people ran after the vehicle, which was by now clearly out of control.

There was a sigh of horror from those watching as the car reached the first slight bend in the road and slewed on to two wheels, its tyres screaming.

'*No* Barty!' Scupper cried, but his voice was lost on the wind and I knew Barty could not hear him, and would not heed even if he heard.

The speeding car passed the goat's field. It hurtled

past the lane that led to our house and the Old Rectory, moving through patches of darkness and light where widely spaced street lamps reflected off the wet road. It almost overturned outside the post office and village store. It approached the sharp bend at the edge of the village. Beyond the bend was a steep twisting hill which led down to the narrow bridge over the river.

It was a tiny distant toy car now, scarcely visible. At the sharp bend it veered over to the wrong side of the road. Then it vanished over the horizon. It was almost as if it had vanished over the edge of the planet.

The explosion, when it came, made people turn away and weep.

'Lord help us,' whispered Auntie. 'Somebody ring for the fire brigade. You! Sam Birtles!' She grabbed the arm of the farm labourer. 'Go and ring the fire brigade at once.'

I stared at her, and felt insane with gratitude for those brusque, familiar tones.

Fenella and I stood motionless for several seconds. Then we picked up two dropped incapacitators and started shakily to unstun villagers who had fallen victim to the aliens. Red Goff was doing the same. The remaining aliens were moving about like robots, dazed, slow and clumsy. Some were rubbing their eyes or foreheads in bewilderment. Parry, who was now standing by the school gate, staggered and said plaintively, 'I don't feel very well. Why do I do this blasted job anyway? I get no thanks for it.'

I stopped unstunning people for a moment and watched her. Then I looked away over the horizon to where flames lit up the sky. Oh Barty. He had taught the most powerful computer in the universe how to choose, and it had chosen to make itself very difficult indeed to mend, this time.

When most of the villagers were back on their feet, and were being helped home or to hospital by large numbers of shocked police officers and the crews of several ambulances, Fenella came and took hold of my hand. Auntie joined us, followed by Julia and Granny Probity. They were distraught, but back to their normal selves.

I looked round for Peter. He was standing quite still, looking down aghast at the clothes he was wearing. I crossed to his side.

'These clothes aren't mine,' he croaked. 'They're someone else's . . . someone else's . . . private property . . .' My heart sank. He shook his head as if to clear it.

'Why did I say that . . . ? That was a strange thing to say . . .' The drenched shirt and pressed grey trousers stuck to him. They were muddy now and no longer neat. He pulled at the soaking material, peeling it away from his skin. 'Sorry Dom. I feel as if I'm just waking up . . .'

I smiled at him. 'You are,' I said, and led him over to join the others.

There were more sirens and flashing lights as even more vehicles from all the emergency services arrived.

'Let's go home.' Auntie put her arm through mine. 'There's nothing more we can do here now.' She looked at Fenella. 'Fenella Brown, why is there always trouble for somebody when you're around?' She glanced at our linked hands and shook her head. 'Dear me. Well, I suppose you'd better come home with us too.'

I bent down to where Scupper was crouched, sobbing, by the fence.

'Scupper, come home with us.' I helped him up. I knew there was nothing I could say that would make him feel better at that moment. Granny Probity looked at his tearstained, contorted face, wrapped her ample arms round him and the cat, and rocked him closely against her like a child.

'There,' she said. 'There there.'

I looked at Red Goff who was standing white faced nearby. Above us, where the unseen, leaping flames still reflected off the low clouds, I realised that the sky was now full of gravity-blasters. There were hardly any Council guards to be seen on the ground. Of Parry and Pearce there was no sign.

'Would you like to come home with us too?' I asked Red Goff. He looked at Fenella for a moment and neither of them spoke.

'Yes, do come,' agreed Julia. Finally Red Goff shook his head.

'No.' He gave a tired smile. 'No thank you. I'm going to visit my mother. I'll be in touch.'

We watched him go, striding over the verge and up the bracken bank, heading for the woods. The flames died down beyond the horizon. Somewhere out there in the dark, an invisible force field, smaller than a human hand but more powerful than the whole world, roamed the damp secret Somerset countryside.

The rain stopped and the stars came out.